Governor Cardell scoffed. "What were we supposed to do? Schedule the battle and notify the people in that neighborhood to not be home at that time?"

"That would have been a hell of a lot better than having them be caught in the middle of your firefight. Forty-seven people are dead and one hundred and seventy-four are wounded from this episode."

The holograms of three men who allegedly hated each other shrugged in unison. "You can't make an omelet without breaking a few eggs," Granja Union President Taft said.

"Blood must be spilled even in the most noble of endeavors," said Count Bishop Rutter.

"They were collateral damage," Governor Cardell said.

"Collateral damage is not acceptable! Innocents dying because the three of you can't talk things out and decide who's in charge doesn't give you the right to kill people," Benedict said. "Even each other."

"You're one to talk, Major. From what I've heard, you killed General Daily to take over his command of the *Behemoth* and today your soldiers killed a member of my church," Count Bishop Rutter said.

"One, Daily is alive." *And quite miserable with his new roommates as per my last several reports,* Benedict added silently. "And as for your mech pilot, he was given warnings about what the consequences of his actions would be, as were you. *You were the one who ordered him to fire on the dropship holding him several hundred feet above the ground. The ship merely lived up to its name and dropped him to avoid being shot at. He and you are responsible for his death, no one else."

"You can't come to our world and start ordering us around," Governor Cardell shouted. "You have no authority here. Worse, you're ignoring my Sway-given dominion over this world."

"You're right about one thing. The Sway did leave you in charge of this world but it appears you were not up to the task," Benedict said.

The governor's hologram stood up and spittles of light cascaded from his open mouth. "How dare you!"

"Prove me wrong. Better yet, tell me how exactly did you lose control?" Benedict said.

"I'll tell you how," Granja President Taft said. "Once news reached Cameroon about the destruction of Earth and the Sway government, the governor here decided he'd rather be a king. Since the government owned the factories and the farms, *his Majesty* announced that what was the government's was now his. Cardell made the workers put in more hours for less pay. When someone would complain about it, *his Majesty* would have them arrested and put in jail. So we workers and farmers joined together around our union to fight against the governor's tyranny."

"I was doing the best I could to hold this world together!" Cardell said, pointing a holographic finger at the union president's hologram.

"Your best was worse than a joke," Count Bishop Rutter said.

BOOKS BY PATRICK THOMAS

THE MURPHY'S LORE™ SERIES
TALES FROM BULFINCHE'S PUB
FOOLS' DAY
THROUGH THE DRINKING GLASS
SHADOW OF THE WOLF
REDEMPTION ROAD
BARTENDER OF THE GODS
NIGHTCAPS
EMPTY GRAVES
THE MUG LIFE

MURPHY'S LORE STARTENDERS™
STARTENDERS
CONSTELLATION PRIZE

MURPHY'S LORE AFTER HOURS™ UNIVERSE:
TERRORBELLE:
FAIRY WITH A GUN
FAIRY RIDES THE LIGHTNING
TERRORBELLE THE UNCONQUERED
AGENT KARVER:
RITES OF PASSAGE *(with John French)*
DEAD TO RITES
HELL'S DETECTIVE:
LORE & DYSORDER
BULLETS & BRIMSTONE *(with John French)*
THE CASE OF THE MOON MANIAC
(graphic novel with Blair Webb)
HEXCRAFT:
BY DARKNESS CURSED
BY INVOCATION ONLY
SOUL FOR HIRE:
GREATEST HITS

XILES:
EXILE & ENTRANCE

BIKINI JONES:
BIKINI JONES VS. THE
BRAINNAPPERS FROM OUT SPACE
BIKINI JONES VS THE SEA MONSTERS
BIKINI JONES VS THE EMPEROR OF PLANET Z

THE JACK GARDNER MYSTERIES
THE ASSASSAINS' BALL *(with John L. French)*

GRIFEIN, BATSQUATCH, & DINGBAT:
CRYPTID FIGHT CLUB

PLAYWORLDS:
AS THE GEARS TURN:
Tales of Steamworld

ANTHOLOGIES AS CO-EDITOR
NEW BLOOD *(with Diane Raetz)*
CAMELOT 13 *(with John L. French)*

DEAR CTHULHU™ SERIES
HAVE A DARK DAY
GOOD ADVICE FOR BAD PEOPLE
CTHULHU KNOWS BEST
WHAT WOULD CTHULHU DO?
CTHULHU HAPPENS
CTHULHU EXPLAINS IT ALL
CTHULHU TAKE THE WHEEL
MYSTIC INVESTIGATORS™ SERIES
MYSTIC INVESTIGATORS
MEAN STREETS
ONCE MORE IN CRIME omnibus
by Patrick Thomas & Diane Raetz
SHADOWS & BRIMSTONE omnibus
by Patrick Thomas & John L. French

AGENTS OF THE ABYSS:
FRANKENSTEIN: MONSTERS OF
THE ABYSS *(with John L. French)*
STARING INTO THE ABYSS: *Editor*
DETECTIVES OF THE ABYSS *(with
John L. French)*

THE 142ND STARBORNE
WE WILL FIGHT IN THE STARS
TO BATTLE A RISING STORM

YA:
THE WILDSIDHE CHRONICLES OMNIBUS
(contributing author)

WRITING AS PATRICK T. FIBBS
YA
EMOTIONAL SUPPORT NIGHTMARE

MIDDLE READERS:
UNDEAD KID DIARIES™:
OVER MY DEAD BODY
IT'S MY PARTY AND I'LL DIE IF I
WANT TO
BABE B. BEAR MYSTERIES™:
BAD HAIR DAY
AIN'T SEEN MUFFIN YET
JOY REAPER CHECKS OUT

YOUNGER READERS:
Ughaboos™ picture books
5 SILLY MONSTERS JUMPING
ON POOR ZED
ON TOP OF A YETI
SOGGY GOES TO THE BEACH
an Ughaboos™ early reader

FUSCHIA: THE MERMAID WHO
LOVED PINK

TO BATTLE A RISING STORM

A Tale of the 142nd Starborne

PATRICK THOMAS

PADWOLF PUBLISHING INC.
WWW.PADWOLF.COM
www.facebook.com/Padwolf

www.patthomas.net

To Battle A Rising Storm
A Tale of the 142nd Starborne

© 2024 regular edition ebook and print editions Patrick Thomas
*(Originally published as a Special Early Edition for backers of the
Rising Storm; The Starborne card game Kickstarter by DPH Games
© 2023 Patrick Thomas)*

The 142nd Starborne and all related characters
and settings are © and ™ Patrick Thomas

edited by John L. French

cover art by Dzaky Ramzy courtesy DPH Games

cover design Roy Mauritsen and Patrick Thomas

142nd Starborne logo Mike McPhail

All rights reserved. This is a work of fiction. Any resemblance to any
person, living or dead, locales or events is purely coincidental. Except for
brief passages used in reviews and criticisms, nothing may be reprinted
without the written consent of the author and publisher.

ISBN 978-1-958310-07-6

First Printing. Printed in the USA

For Dan Hundycz.

*Thanks for bringing
the 142nd into a new frontier.*

CAST OF CHARACTERS:

On *Behemoth*:
　　Major Hans Benedict: Leader of the 142nd Starborne and *Behemoth*, the last remaining Colossus class star destroyer in the universe. Master Sapper.
　　Captain Shanna Morales: Second-in-command of the 142nd Starborne.
　　Colonel Bai Zhang: Third-in-command of the 142nd Starborne. Intelligence expert.
　　Otto Daily: Former general. Was relieved of command of *Behemoth* and the 142nd Starborne for willingness to senselessly cause the death of over one hundred thousand civilians and all those under his command.
　　Emissary Sarah Tungsten: Representative of the Sway Government stationed onboard *Behemoth*. Possibly the highest-ranking member of the civilian government left alive.
　　Sergeant Ajani Opara: Soldier and former interworld supervisor of the Granja union.
　　Private Ricco Jonas: Novice sapper. Descendant of the Renfields who served Dracula. His Grandfather escaped the purge of Transylvania by the Sway.

On the planet Cameroon:
　　Governor Hobe Cardell: Sway-appointed governor of the Cameroon colony. Head of the planetary police force.
　　Donavan Rutter: Count Bishop and Exalted High Reverend of the Sangre Temple on Cameroon. Worships and lives by the teachings of Dracula.
　　Lars Taft: The Granja Union President on Cameroon, representing workers and farmers.

1

"General Daily sends his regards, traitor," the assassin whispered, stabbing down to the mattress.

It was the first time Captain Bert Holland had attempted to kill anyone. He took perverse pleasure in the prospect of taking of another man's life. Especially this man.

Now he just had to complete his mission and find what Major Benedict stole.

One moment Holland was turning to begin his search. The next his nose was broken as he fell face-first onto the floor. The attack had happened so fast Holland was still processing his smashed nasal cartilage when he realized something had grabbed hold of his ankle and yanked him forcefully to the deck.

Before he could either reach a hand up to his broken nose or turn to see who had attacked him, his arms were pulled behind him. The pain in his nose was soon dwarfed by that of both his shoulders being dislocated as his wrists were hogtied to his ankles like he was in an old-fashioned Western instead of serving on the Colossus class star destroyer *Behemoth*.

"It's always nice to hear from old friends. Why don't you tell Daily I said hi back? Better yet, I'll tell him myself," Major Hans Benedict said. "Right after you and I have a conversation, Mr. Holland."

Bert Holland always considered himself a tough guy so he spat out, "That's Captain Holland, traitor."

"Not anymore. Consider yourself dishonorably discharged."

"I don't recognize your authority, Benedict."

"You were the one stupid enough to not check before you stabbed a pillow. And whether you recognize my authority doesn't matter one bit to me." Benedict pulled the knife out of his boot and pressed the tip to Bert Holland's throat.

As a chilling wave of terror crashed against the shores of his mind, Bert Holland realized he wasn't anything like a tough guy. "You can't. It's against military law to torture a fellow soldier of the Host."

"Then it's fortunate that I've already told you that you're no longer a soldier."

Bert Holland's Adam's apple trembled. "It's also against military law to torture a civilian."

"It is. How fortunate that you aren't one," Benedict said.

"But if I'm not a soldier, that makes me civilian. There are only two choices."

"There are several other choices. Military law has an entirely different set of regulations regarding what can be done to spies and assassins."

Bert Holland craned his neck back and looked up to see the man with short-cropped hair and graying temples looking down at him and smiling as if he had been given the most wonderful present in the world.

"Shit."

Benedict nodded. "I'm certain that you'll do that along the way. Let's get this over with quickly because I tend to be cranky when I don't get a full six hours of beauty sleep. Although I already know the answer, let's start with who sent you."

Bert Holland started screaming, stopping only to blubber out some answers.

2

"Holland told you everything?" Captain Shana Morales said.

Major Hans Benedict nodded. "Even a few things I didn't ask."

"And you never actually hurt him?"

Benedict shrugged. "I wouldn't say that. Holland has a broken nose, two dislocated shoulders, and a knife prick on his neck, but no other physical injuries."

"Sometimes a threat holds a greater terror than what will actually happen," Colonel Bai Zhang said.

"How did you know he was coming?" Captain Shayna Morales's said.

Benedict shook his head. "I didn't."

"Then why were you sleeping under your bed with your head and feet reversed?" Morales said.

"I'm a sapper," Benedict said, as if the answer should have been obvious.

Confused, Morales tilted her head.

"A sapper's job is to infiltrate enemy lines to do what needs to be done," Zhang said. "As such, the major has had to contemplate many scenarios that might not occur to the average soldier so, even in his everyday life, he has put measures in place to counter them before they occur."

"So you construct a blanket doppelgänger in your bed and sleep under it because there is a chance that someone might try to kill you when you're while you're asleep?" Morales said.

Benedict nodded. "Yes. Although I built a dummy doppelgänger. Saves time."

"And you keep your head at the opposite end so that if they use a gun it would go through the bed," Morales said.

"Yes, but I armor-plated the underside of my bunk. The head–foot switch is in case they use armor–piercing shells. I'd be more likely to survive a foot wound than a head shot."

"Maybe I should start sleeping under my bed," Morales said.

"I wouldn't. After this, any would–be assassins on board will be checking for that . Fortunately, Benedict used a different method than I do, so I won't have to change," said Bhang.

"Where do you sleep?" Morales said.

"Him telling you would defeat the purpose," Benedict said. "The important question is, how will this getting out affect the crew?"

"We know there are those on board who don't agree with our taking control to stop Daily from killing us all," Morales said.

"Weird way to treat the people who saved their lives but to each their own," Zhang said. "We make sure the rumor mill knows Benedict took down the assassin and left him in tears."

"Enough people certainly witnessed his blubbering," Morales sat.

"But how do we show people that we are still in charge?" Benedict said.

"We keep doing what we are doing. Run this ship and the 142nd Starborne. As my grandmother used to say, fake it until you make it," Morales said. "Except we really *are* in charge. If I had known how hard this was, I would have thought twice about agreeing to be second in command."

"We could promote you to General if you like," Zhang teased.

Morales shook her head. "Because we *took* control of the ship, we all agreed never to take a higher rank so what we did was more of relieving an unfit superior rather than a coup."

"And to focus on the day-to-day, we will be arriving at the planet Cameroon in just over forty hours," Zhang said. "We are in desperate need of restocking armaments after ending the glob threat on Rushmore. In addition to Private Hugh, we lost sixteen of our twenty battle mechs and are down to forty-one percent of our drones. Prior to Earth's destruction, Cameroon was home to the Sway's main manufacturing plants for both battle mech and drone ordnance.

"Before Earth's destruction, all *Behemoth* would've had to do was make orbit and load up the new mechs and drones onto our harpy dropships as long as our paperwork was in order. With the Sway's central government on Earth destroyed, getting restocked may end up being a bit more challenging," Zhang said.

"I'd also like to restock our larders with fresh meat, fruit, and vegetables. We are nearly out of what Rushmore colony gifted us after we saved their herds. Plus, we should buy all the spices they will sell us. The nutrient vats produce and recycle what we laughingly refer to as food which, while nourishing, tastes like crud. Anything we can get to improve the taste after the fresh stuff runs out would be a gift from the heavens. The locals will likely want payment of some sort."

"Will they even accept digital Sway currency? Or have they developed their own? Or like some of the worlds we've seen gone to a barter system," Morales said.

"Whichever is, we'll have to figure it out. Although the truth of the matter is unless they've changed how they manufacture, the mechs and drones are useless to them," Benedict said.

"Useless to us too without the activation code," Zhang said.

"The thimble can't bypass that?" Morales said. The thimble was the ultimate military controller. It had previously belonged to the former five-star general Daily who was tricked into giving control of it over to Major Benedict. Benedict, Morales, and Zhang objected to the wholesale slaughter of the *Behemoth*'s crew and the death of over a hundred thousand people on the planet they would've had to leave in order to do Daily's kamikaze run. All of that to save a couple hundred high-ranking Sway who had caused the conflagration on Earth and killed billions.

They saved the Diamondhead colony, Daily was imprisoned in the brig, and the three of them had taken over running the last Colossus class warship in the Host fleet. The situation was unprecedented in the annals of military history as they had performed their mutiny in service to the Host rather than against it.

"The thimble can take control once the mechs and drones

are on, but it can't be used to activate them. There were rumored to be five or less thimbles in existence. The mere activation of ordinary mechs and drones was not a task considered worthy of someone who rated a thimble. They would send out the same Inspector General for each round of activations to make sure no one on the planet of manufacture could activate them, reducing the risk of a disloyal faction taking control of their weaponry or using them in a rebellion."

"Ironic since they would consider what we did a rebellion. The ruling council of the Sway make Benedict here look trusting," Zhang said. "Unfortunately, the only person we know of who has the activation code is Daily. Who as we know is obviously not favorably inclined towards any of us."

"Judging by him sending one of his former staff to kill Hans, I'd have to agree with you on that," Morales said.

"Holland didn't visit Dailey. How did he issue the kill order on me?" Benedict said.

"Daily was allowed three visitors. One was Colonel Ernest Robiten. They basically used a variety of body parts to tap out a message using Morse code which the guards on monitor duty missed. We only noticed when reviewing the footage," Zhang said.

"No more visitors for Daily."

"Agreed," Morales said. "How do we get the code?"

"Daily is unlikely to simply give it to us," Zhang said.

"Question is what does the general want badly enough to trade the code for?" Benedict said.

"I guess we could always ask him," Morales joked.

"I was thinking the same thing," Benedict said.

3

tto Daily immediately noticed two things when he was startled awake. One was that his cell was pitch dark. Even during his sleep cycle, there were always small red lights lit around Brig A.

The second was that something cold and hard was pressed up against his jugular.

"I understand you sent me a message so I thought I'd responded in person."

"You eluded the Reaper yet again did you, Benedict? A pity that a traitor such as you is rewarded so unjustly and so often by the universe. I guess you finally grew the balls you needed to kill me. I'm truly surprised it took you this long."

"Actually, I came to ask you a question–what would you like in exchange for the new ordnance activation code?"

Daily chuckled. "That's simple. Return of my thimble and restoration of command of *Behemoth* to me."

"How about asking for something that we might actually give you."

"Benedict, as long as I'm locked in a cell, there is nothing you can possibly offer me other than my freedom. I'm not going give you those codes so you might as well slit my throat and be done with it."

"I'm not here to slit your throat. Just running some diagnostic tests on your general health for the docs." Benedict pulled away a medical scanner that worked by pressing it up against someone's neck. "I just thought I'd give you a chance to work with us and help out the 142nd and maybe get a little something in return."

"I'll dance naked through the gates of Hell before I do anything that would help you, Benedict."

"So noted. I'm also here to tell you that you're getting two new roommates."

"Are you mad? The cell is barely twelve by twelve. It's not

large enough for one person, let alone three."

Hans Benedict smiled and motioned with his hand. The full lights came on. The cell door opened. Two soldiers came in and removed the former general's bed. Six more entered, each pair carrying military-grade cots which they stacked atop each other to make a triple bunk bed. It was bolted together using power tools so there was no way to take it apart by hand.

The former general took in the new arrangement of beds and then glared at Benedict. "You're serious?"

"As a sniper," Benedict replied.

"There are more than a dozen empty cells on this block alone."

"I'm aware and I will be happy to relocate your new roommates to separate cells once you share with us the new weapons activation code."

The general narrowed his eyes. "So that's how it is? You're hardly going to break a soldier of my caliber by giving me roommates."

"Perhaps." Benedict nodded at the soldier standing sentry at the open door who then motioned outside the cell. Two men were marched into the cell.

"I believe you're familiar with former captain Bert Holland and former colonel Ernest Robiten. We were foolish enough to allow you to have Robiten as a visitor. You took advantage of our kindness and issued a kill order on me to Holland."

Dailey grinned. "Putting me in with two of the finest soldiers on this ship. I should be thanking you."

"We'll see but I do have to point out that they are no longer soldiers thanks to listening to you. I imagine there's going to be quite some resentment coming your way. Both of them will be serving a life sentence."

"They are officers and gentlemen."

"Not any longer. And neither are you. It may take them a bit to realize it, but you're no longer their superior officer. The three of you are now all the same, no better or worse, no higher or lower ranking than each other. That means they no longer have to obey your orders. They're both younger and in better shape than you are so I suspect you might be following *their* orders before too long. Have a wonderful day, all of you," Benedict said, stepping out of the cell. After he nodded to the soldiers to shut the door, he turned to watch the former captain and colonel glare at their former general.

Daily's expression transformed from confident to nervous.

4

Sappers tended to sneak in wherever they went in order to complete their mission and get out, preferably with no one ever realizing they had been there. Being a sapper had shaped Major Hans Benedict's leadership style. Upon arriving at the Cameroon colony, he would have preferred performing recognizance before announcing the arrival of *Behemoth* and her crew.

That wasn't an option as they detected multiple distress calls regarding a firefight happening in the residential center of the capital city of Depot. It had been named that because it was originally a weapons depot and as the Cameroon colony city grew, the name stuck.

Three groups were firing weapons at each other without regard for the risk of civilian casualties. The three sides were employing mechs—two P-1s and an unknown model—which were basically tanks with arms and legs and designed to emulate the movements of a person. To Major Benedict, collateral damage was a foul word and unacceptable. Something Benedict liked even less was getting involved in a firefight without knowing who the sides were and why the conflict was happening.

Innocents were in multiple lines of fire, so in this case there was no other conscionable option.

Ten harpy dropships were launched and swiftly arrived at the city center. The harpies hovered out of weapons range.

"Attention combatants, this is Captain Diya Patel in Harpy Alpha Nine," came a message on the general broadcast channel and the speakers of all ten harpy dropships. "By the authority of the 142nd Starborne, cease all hostilities and power down your mechs immediately. All combat participants are ordered to stand down and place their weapons on the ground, then step back with their hands above their heads. Failure to comply will resort will result in severe and possibly fatal repercussions."

The firing of weapons halted but otherwise Patel's orders were ignored.

"Alpha Nine, this is Sway Governor Hobe Cardell," came a man's voice over the communication system. "By the authority invested in me by the Sway government, I hereby assume command of the 142nd Starborne. You will follow my commands and destroy the two terrorist groups and the soldiers that stand with them."

"Apologies Governor Cardell, but that's not how things work. The 142nd Starborne answered to a Sway government that no longer exists. And even if it still did, you are giving an illegal order. Planetary governors can only request assistance, they cannot order Host forces. You have a police force under your command."

"Who do you think is in the blue P-1 mech? I reject your assertion that the Sway government does not exist because I am its representative and I am still here, so either take out the Sangre and Granja rebel forces or stand down and stay out of our way."

"So what I hear you saying Governor is that you want the planetary police to be the first combatants we open fire upon. Is that correct?" asked Captain Patel.

Cardell's deep inhalation was clear over the comm. "Captain Patel, I can assure you the Sway is in the right in this situation."

"Do you know what's better than assurances, Governor? Proof. And doing what you were told to do would prove what you're saying, so tell your forces to stand down."

"Very well but we will not power off our mechs or put our weapons down until the Sangre and the Granja do the same. I will not have my people be sitting ducks for these murderous terrorists."

"Harpy Alpha Nine, this is Granja Union President Lars Taft and I can assure you we are in the right as we are only fighting for our members' rights and well–being by striking back against the tyranny placed upon them by the tyrant Cardell. However, to show our good intentions, we will also cease fire and pull our G-1 mech back. For the moment at least."

"Harpy dropship, this is Count Bishop Donavan Rutter, Exalted High Reverend of the Sangre Temple on Cameroon. We do not recognize the Sway's authority nor do we recognize that of the Host or the 142nd Starborne. We Sangre answer to a higher authority, that of the Lord of life and death, Vlad himself. Interfere with us and we will destroy you as we will them. Congregant Huber, continue your attack!"

The red mech, which appeared to be an exact copy of the planetary police's blue P-1 mech except for a coat of scarlet paint, opened fire on the steel mech which looked like it had been put together in the dark by a team of kindergartners who had eaten nothing but a steady diet of chocolate and espresso for three days.

The cessation of hostilities brought about by the sudden appearance of the 142nd Starborne's dropship was over.

"You were all warned," Captain Patel said. "Front gunner, launch the harpoon on the red mech."

"Yes Captain," said Private Giang. The harpoon was a high-grade electric magnet supplemented by industrial pincers that was fired at the top of the red mech and latched onto it. A moment later, Alpha Nine took off straight up into the sky, taking the red P-1 mech and its one-person crew with it.

"Red Mech, you have been captured. Power down your weapons and prepare to be taken into custody. Failure to do so may result in injury or death," Captain Patel broadcast.

"Congregant Huber, this is Count Bishop Rutter. That dropship is in range of your weapons. Fire and destroy it!"

Huber sat in the pilot pod in the center of the ten-foot-tall mech. The arms of the P-1 were able to swivel in any direction that wouldn't result in the mech successfully shooting itself. Both arm guns swiveled up to fire at the underside of the Harpy dropship.

After calculating a downward trajectory that would avoid civilian casualties, Captain Patel hit a button, turning off the harpoon electromagnet and releasing the pincers. The red mech went into free fall, landing in the center of a large cross street, its impact making a small crater and smashing the red P-1 to pieces. Huber did not survive as he was torn into far smaller and mushier pieces.

"Idiots," Patel whispered to herself. She turned on her mic for all the harpy speakers. "Not a terribly bright idea to fire at a ship that's holding one off the ground. The two remaining mechs have one minute to power down and the combatants have thirty seconds to put their guns on the ground and back away from them or we will open fire on all combatants and destroy the remaining mechs." Switching to private broadcast, she said, "Dropships advance and surround the area."

Ten harpies moving into position in the sky above them was a frightening and humbling sight to the combatants, especially as they watched their side gunners aiming at them.

This time everyone obeyed. Four dropships landed, dispersing armed soldiers who quickly took the now unarmed combatants into custody, using restraint bands to cuff their hands behind their backs as each was searched for more weapons.

Which is how the *Battle of Front Street* ended with no victory for any of the participants.

5

ajor Hans Benedict stared at the three holograms and had to force himself not to call them idiots as that wouldn't be terribly diplomatic. If this was the best Cameroon could muster, the planet was in for some very tough times. "Would you lot explain to me how things have degenerated on Cameroon to the point where the lot of you are playing soldier in the streets and endangering innocent civilians?"

Governor Cardell scoffed. "What were we supposed to do? Schedule the battle and notify the people in that neighborhood to not be home at that time?"

"That would have been a hell of a lot better than having them be caught in the middle of your firefight. Forty-seven people are dead and one hundred and seventy-four are wounded from this episode."

The holograms of three men who allegedly hated each other shrugged in unison. "You can't make an omelet without breaking a few eggs," Granja Union President Taft said.

"Blood must be spilled even in the most noble of endeavors," said Count Bishop Rutter.

"They were collateral damage," Governor Cardell said.

"Collateral damage is not acceptable! Innocents dying because the three of you can't talk things out and decide who's in charge doesn't give you the right to kill people," Benedict said. "Even each other."

"You're one to talk, Major. From what I've heard, you killed General Daily to take over his command of the *Behemoth* and today your soldiers killed a member of my church," Count Bishop Rutter said.

"One, Daily is alive." *And quite miserable with his new roommates as per my last several reports,* Benedict added silently. "And as for your mech pilot, he was given warnings about what the consequences of his actions would be, as were you. *You* were the one who ordered him to fire on the dropship holding him several hundred feet above the ground. The ship merely lived up to its name and dropped him to avoid being shot at. He and you are responsible for his death, no one else."

"You can't come to our world and start ordering us around," Governor Cardell shouted. "You have no authority here. Worse, you're ignoring my Sway-given dominion over this world."

"You're right about one thing. The Sway did leave you in charge of this world but it appears you were not up to the task," Benedict said.

The governor's hologram stood up and spittles of light cascaded from his open mouth. "How dare you!"

"Prove me wrong. Better yet, tell me how exactly did you lose control?" Benedict said.

"I'll tell you how," Granja President Taft said. "Once news reached Cameroon about the destruction of Earth and the Sway government, the governor here decided he'd rather be a king. Since the government owned the factories and the farms, *his Majesty* announced that what was the government's was now his. Cardell made the workers put in more hours for less pay. When someone would complain about it, *his Majesty* would have them arrested and put in jail. So we workers and farmers joined together around our union to fight against the governor's tyranny."

"I was doing the best I could to hold this world together!" Cardell said, pointing a holographic finger at the union president's hologram.

"Your best was worse than a joke," Count Bishop Rutter said. "But I should thank you because you made people turn back to the Church of Blood."

"Which leads to another question. Wasn't the Sangre Temple outlawed by the Sway?" Benedict said.

"Oh yes. We were mightily persecuted by the Sway and Prime Minister Van Helsing. He could not stand that King Dracula of Transylvania was the only one to ever stand successfully against the Sway. But punishment and persecution can be endured, so the one true church survived underground, much like our Lord and

Savior Dracula was often forced to. I take the Sway's destruction as a powerful sign that King Dracula will return to us."

"Van Helsing destroyed King Dracula and Transylvania a long time ago," Benedict said.

"Transylvania, the last free country in the world, lives on in the hearts of free people everywhere in the galaxy. And our Lord and Savior Dracula was said to have been destroyed many times before, including by Van Helsing. Dracula will rise again and remake this and every other world in his image as he once did with Transylvania."

"Assuming he was alive before, he's dead now. Earth is one vast wasteland," Benedict said.

"Who said that Dracula had to be on Earth? As the highest ranking representative of the Church of Blood, I claim dominion by right of being Dracula's lawful heir. These others and everyone else on this world must join the Sangre and accept Dracula as their Lord and Savior. If they do this, they will all be treated fairly. If they don't then they will fall before us!" Rutter emphasized his point by leaning in close to the camera so his light construct was mostly head and fangs.

"Nice dental work. Trying to convince the rank–and–file that you are a vampire like old Vlad?" Benedict said.

"I am all too aware of the Sway's standing order that any vampire not in military service to the Host was to be immediately executed upon their discovery. But the Sway is no more, so I do not have to hide what I am any longer."

"Nice try, Rutter, but I've met vampires and you, sir, may be bloodsucking scum but you are no vampire. You simply paid a dentist to sculpt your teeth into that shape. I have no problem with folks worshiping however they want to. My problem begins whenever someone tries to force their religious beliefs onto someone else. My objections only increase when they are trying to conquer a colony by force."

"The Books of Blood, which hold the words and teaching of King Vlad, tell us that the strong must ever rule the weak and that includes those whose faith and belief is weak. Now the Sway is weak but we Sangre are strong and thus their time is done and ours begins."

"Neither of you can do anything without being carried on the backs of the working men and women of this world. For once, the workers are going to control the means of production," Union President Taft said.

"Right now, I have neither the time nor inclination to explain to you lot the difference between governing and ruling but I will tell you this much. I will not let you shoot up innocent people. How did you three get a hold of mechs? They are supposed to be nonworking without the activation code."

"Our police force has a number of P-1 mechs to protect the people since the Sway decided not to house troops in the same place where they made weapons. Our P-1s aren't quite military grade but are impressive nevertheless," Governor Cardell said.

"You *had* a number," Count Bishop Rutter said. "But the Sangre have managed to take control of about half the P-1s you once had."

"And painted them all red," Taft said. "Subpar job too, but that's what you get when you don't use union workers."

"So, Governor, you had lousy security and Rutter's congregants stole half your drones. Got it. That still doesn't explain how the Granja have a style of mech I've never seen before," Benedict said. "In your communication with Captain Patel, you called it a G-1."

"Short for Granja-1. Benedict, I'm not sure if you're familiar with country and western music from back in the 20th century on Earth. There was a man named Cash who had a song where he bragged about stealing a car from the factory he worked at one piece at a time. That's pretty much what we did. Our mech was built over a period of years. One bit here, another bit there. When the Sway upgraded models, we took the parts they scrapped. We made different models work together and figured out a way to bypass the control board. Weapon systems were too heavily guarded and too operating system dependent for us to acquire any parts so we built pneumatic cannons that shoot rivets and are manually controlled. The entire G-1 mech is manually controlled instead of by software. Ours are a bit slower than theirs, but far more durable as they are military-grade.

Benedict didn't say it out loud but he was impressed. The Sway was careful to keep the engineers who designed their weapons on different worlds than the ones where they were built as a security measure. People here had figured out a workaround. A regular military mech would run circles around the jury-rigged model the Granja were fielding but its pneumatic cannons used a helium mix. The rivets could rip holes in police armor that was rated for civil disturbances, not the battlefield.

Unfortunately, the Sway control boards in those P-1s would not be affected by the Host thimble as they were in a parallel chain of command, so the military-issued "magic wand" was worthless on them.

"Since the planetary police also are listed as having a number of drones, half of which I fully expect are in the hands of Rutter's people–" The governor glared and the Count Bishop smirked, showing his fake fangs. "–I fully expect that no drones will be used on or near civilians or there will be consequences. We have confiscated the three mechs used on Front Street but let's move on to the reason for our visit. We are here to take delivery of your completed military mechs and drones," Benedict said.

Considering they were enemies, the holograms of the three men exchanged wary glances on faces that had suddenly shifted to try and show no emotion.

"I'm afraid that just won't be possible," Governor Cardell said.

"Why is that?" Benedict said.

"A lack of paperwork, obviously. I'm not authorized to release any product without the proper requisition forms."

"That should hardly be a problem." Benedict looked off to the side where Morales and Zhang sat out of view of the hologram. Zhang nodded and pressed his screen. "Even though you received it previously, you've just been sent another copy of the requisition forms for the ordnance."

There were, in fact, two prior requisitions sent. The first was legitimate and sent prior to the conflagration of Earth and had been signed by then General Daily, for the regular X-1 models and some of the new X-3 models which used a three-person team–a pilot and two gunners. The second was not quite as legitimate as they had made it themselves and it was signed by Benedict instead of Daily for a significantly higher number.

Governor Cardell looked down, presumably at a screen of his own. "I'm afraid, Major Benedict, that I cannot recognize you as an authorized signer as you do not have the military authority, and as a mere major, you do not have the rank as all military requisitions must be approved by a general."

"We can circle back to my authority. The first requisition is dated prior to Earth's destruction and is signed not only by General Daily but by the Sway Council's Quartermaster on Earth."

"But with that destruction, we have no way of verifying this."

"We can verify its transmission to you and that you received it with plenty of time to have verified it when such a thing was still possible," Benedict countered.

"Be that as it may–"

"And according to Host regulation 2016a, section 7, subsection 18 any Sway authority who ignores a lawful military order may be removed from their position if their action directly interferes with an active military operation," Benedict said.

Cardell sighed. "That gets you your dozen X-1s and six X-3s and twenty-five fighter drones. It does nothing to get you the additional fifty–two mech and one hundred and twelve drones on this cute little requisition you wrote up and signed yourself," the governor said.

"Whether or not you recognize my authority is moot. I am the commander of the sole remaining Colossus class star destroyer in the galaxy. The 142nd Starborne is also the last fully intact and space–worthy military command, which means not giving us what I've requisitioned is interfering with a military operation."

"We don't even have that many–"

"Governor, don't try to feed me bullshit and tell me it's chocolate pudding. We know for a fact that you had the parts necessary and completed work assembling exactly the number of X mechs and fighter drones that we requisitioned."

The holographic governor's eyebrows shot up. "How could you possibly know that? Our production is classified."

"Governor, your first mistake during these negotiations was trying to lie to me. Your second was confirming my numbers."

What Benedict left out was what the governor should have already figured out. The 142nd Starborne's tech tactile team of hackers had already infiltrated the Governor's system. The Sway had been paranoid, careful, and very aware of the vulnerability of technology so they did not have one central computing system because it would be too vulnerable to attack. Every section of the government and military had its own isolated system with a separate system used for communication. It was impossible to use the communication system to get into anything else. That meant the tech tactical team or T3 had to get themselves on-site to get into the governor's system. They weren't sappers but they were far better than most. They had been in and out of the government building and the system with no one being the wiser. They did the same to the Granja and the Sangre Temple systems but those two factions stored far less sensitive data on their systems. T3 reported that they had been impressed with the Granja's system defenses, meaning that only did they have people with the skills to repurpose parts to build a modified mech but they had hackers who knew enough to build unique cyber defenses for their system.

"Even if we gave them to you, they'd be useless without the activation code," Cardell said.

"That's not your worry. Just deliver the ordnance and let me worry about activation," Benedict said.

"No," Governor Cardell said.

"Very well. You leave me no choice but to place you under military arrest," Benedict said.

"What?!" Governor Cardell sputtered.

The hologram of the governor was spun around by a new figure, Captain Leon Juma, a sapper in the 142nd Starborne who had managed to walk right into the governor's office with a squad of soldiers at his back. Juma placed Cardell's hands behind his back and cuffed them together.

"Wait. It's not that I don't want to give them to you," Cardell said.

"Hobe, don't you say a word," the hologram of Count Bishop Rutter said.

"Keep your yap shut, Cardell," Union President Taft's hologram yelled.

Cardell tried to negotiate. "If you remove me from office, who's going to take my place?"

"I suppose our Sway Emissary. She does outrank you," Benedict said.

"Does that mean the Emissary will have the military backing of the 142nd Starborne?" Count Bishop Rutter said.

Benedict nodded. "She would."

"You might as well tell him," Union President Taft said. The hologram of the head of the Sangre Temple grumbled but otherwise didn't say anything.

"Tell me what?" Benedict said.

"We don't have the ordnance."

"What do you mean you don't have it?" Benedict asked. "What happened to them?"

"They were being stored in the warehouse awaiting pickup and then the conflagration happened and we realized that no one was likely to come to get them. Without the activation codes, they were useless to us so we just left them there. In hindsight, we probably should've been more diligent with our security because someone cut the surveillance feed and hacked into the onsite system, looping footage of the mechs standing silently with the drones laid out around them. We didn't keep a guard inside because the ordnance was of no use to anyone. Then one of these two traitors stole them all."

"King Vlad states that those who make false statements

against the true believers best be ready to pay for their lies in blood," Rutter said.

"It would have been against union regulations and no member of the Granja would have done that," Taft said.

"So what you're saying is enough firepower to level the city of Depot is missing and none of you have any idea where it is?" Benedict said.

"You're making it sound worse than it is," the governor said, his hands still bound behind his back.

"I don't think I am. If all of you are telling the truth, that means someone else on this planet is in control of the firepower and all three of you let it happen."

Three holograms muttered a bit but reluctantly agreed.

"Captain Juma, take the restraints off the governor."

Cardell's body practically melted into a puddle in relief. "Thank you, Major…"

"At least for now. The 142nd Starborne is going to do a full search of all your facilities. I'm also going to send you each a diplomatic liaison, to whom you will extend all due courtesy until this matter is solved to my satisfaction," Benedict said.

"Are you planning to use these liaisons to replace us after you arrest us?" Count Bishop Rutter said. "Because my congregants won't stand for that."

"My membership has the right to duly elect their leader," Taft said.

"No one is being replaced or arrested. *Yet.* But if any of you are lying and have hidden the missing ordnance, you will be taken into custody along with any accomplices. On the other hand, if any of you know something you don't want to share in front of the others, contact me and let me know. If someone can give me information that leads to finding the missing ordnance, I will be more kindly disposed toward them. Benedict out."

With that, Captain Shana Morales cut the holographic feed, as she, Zhang, and Benedict exchanged worried glances.

6

"So the three of you are clear on your mission?" Major Hans Benedict said.

The three people sitting across the desk from him bobbed their heads in unison.

"Any questions?"

"Plenty," Emissary Sarah Tungsten said. "You want us to infiltrate while acting as diplomats and search for the missing mechs and drones. Later, we may subtly or not so subtly take over from the inside. I don't think it's going to be anywhere near that simple."

"Things that need doing rarely are but Captain Morales, Colonel Zhang, and I went through *Behemoth's* personnel records with a fine-tooth comb. We all believe that the three of you are our best chance to end this civil war with the least amount of bloodshed. Preferably none."

"I understand that, Major. Truly, I do, but why are they going to listen to the three of us?" Emissary Tungsten straightened her black robes then adjusted her hood and ceremonial visor.

"Because technically, each of you outranks the leaders in these three organizations. For instance, our novice sapper Private Ricco Jonas is descended from the Roma Renfields who served King Dracula. By old Transylvanian law and the rules of the Sangre Temple, a renfield outranks any other human in the hierarchy."

"While that may be true, King Dracula and Transylvania fell to the Sway almost seventy years before I was born. I have no true ranking. The Sway erased Transylvania and the surrounding territories. I've never met any of my family who served Vlad because they were all killed during the purge. I've never attended a single Sangre service."

"And with good reason as the Sway outlawed the church so they had to worship underground. With Earth destroyed, they've obviously come out of the shadows," Benedict said.

"But I don't know anything about the religion," Private Jonas said.

"An intense debriefing with Colonel Zhang will rectify that. You are a sapper, you can do this. It turns out a renfield has a great deal of power in the religion, far more than Count Bishop Rutter."

"That's fine and good for Ricco but I haven't worked for the union since the host drafted me," Sergeant Ajani Opara said.

"But you grew up and worked as a farmer in northern Nigeria where you joined the union and rose through the ranks until you were an interworld supervisor, correct?" Benedict said.

Sergeant Ajani Opara nodded. "But I left that position when I was drafted."

"The Host had an agreement with the Granja. Any union members who are drafted get to keep their position and title until their term of service is completed at which point they go back to that position so you are still an interworld supervisor which means you technically outrank a planetary president."

"But each colony's union is supposed to have a certain level of autonomy. I can't just barge in and start giving orders and expect them to be followed," Sergeant Opara said.

"Which is why we have our people going through the Granja bylaws for loopholes."

"Permission to speak freely sir," Sergeant Opara said.

Benedict nodded. "Granted, Sergeant."

"I'm fairly certain that armed insurrection is against Granja union bylaws but that hasn't stopped them from participating. I don't know that a rule or point of order from me is going to win the day here."

"Agreed, but it might contribute to a better conclusion than letting the people of this world fight it out."

"Not wanting to beat a zombie here, but I need to add my own insights to those of the sergeant and the private," Emissary Tungsten said. "While an emissary ranks just below the Sway High Council, that doesn't mean we have a lot of practical power.

By the protocols, I outrank you and former General Daily but were I to give either of you a direct order, you would not have to obey it unless I could back it up with either a violation of a major law, a risk to Sway governmental security, or a clear and present danger. Or, of course, a direct order from the Sway High Council which can no longer be invoked."

"True, but our ranking is in the Host, not the Sway. The planetary governor and his chain of command are all civilian government and by the laws of the Sway, would have to obey your order regardless of the reason," Benedict said.

"With the Sway government destroyed they really don't have any reason to follow my orders," Emissary Tungsten said.

"Very true, however, Cardell is using the argument that he is in charge by order of the Sway. If he blatantly ignores that rule of law, he will no longer be able to claim he has the right of succession. That will undoubtedly be jumped on by the other two factions," Benedict said. "This will not be an easy task for any of you. I don't know which of these factions would do the best job ruling this planet. My personal opinion is none of them would do a good job but they are the people who have mustered the forces to attempt to claim power here on Cameroon.

"Our job is to stop these three from destroying Cameroon and the people they want to govern. There are too many colony worlds out there that need our help for us to stay in one place too long. We need to make sure there is a system in place that will assure that this world can rule itself without harming its citizens. The missions given to the three of you are crucial parts of that. I appreciate all of you stepping up but if any of you have any misgivings, speak up now because tomorrow is too late."

Sergeant Ajani Opara and Private Ricco Jonas shot up and came to attention while Emissary Sarah Tungsten elegantly stood.

"Sir, we are prepared to do whatever is necessary to help this world," Sergeant Ajani Opara said.

"Yes, we are sir," Private Ricco Jonas said.

"I too will do whatever is within my abilities," Emissary Sarah Tungsten said.

Major Hans Benedict stood and saluted the two officers, then turned and nodded to the emissary.

"Good. Now the lot of you get to your debriefings because you're going planetside in the morning."

7

"**W**elcome to the Sangre Temple, Private Jonas," said a man in red robes, obviously a lackey.

"Where is Count Bishop Rutter?"

"The Count Bishop sends his regards and apologies that he could not meet you himself, but I am Deacon White. The Count Bishop bade me bring you to his office to await his convenience."

This wasn't boding well. It seemed that Major Hans Benedict's idea of all due respect and that of Rutter differed greatly.

Jonas remembered the stories his grandfather told him of his time growing up in Transylvania. The man had only survived because of King Vlad. Dracula may have been many dark and evil things but he was very protective of his Roma guards and his renfield servants. The vampire king had sent their spouses and children to shelter elsewhere when he first suspected that the Sway was coming for him.

If Private Jonas wanted to be taken seriously this would not do at all.

"Rutter dares insult me like this?" Private Jonas said.

"That's Count Bishop Rutter, Private," Deacon White said.

"Did you just dare presume to make eye contact with me, White?"

"Again, you will address me as Deacon White."

"You will answer to whatever I choose to call you, as will Rutter. Now that you've added insult upon insult, you best tell me where Rutter is."

"I'm afraid Count Bishop Rutter does not wish that information shared." White met Private Jonas's eyes but lowered his eyes at the sapper's glare.

"Do you think I give a damn what Rutter wants? A renfield has asked you a question and if I have to ask it again, I will defrock you."

The deacon looked up in shock. "Excuse me?"

"Don't you know the rules of the church you serve in? As the personal servants of the great King Vlad Dracula, a renfield is second to no one in the church save a vampire or Dracula himself. My heritage is listed in the Book of Genealogy. I am the great-grandson of Armando Renfield." Renfields were given the last name "Renfield" in honor of their service. As connections to Transylvania could be deadly after the great purge, Ricco's family had changed their name. Jonas held up a printout from the church's book of genealogy, proving what he said. White took it and read it, turning paler with each line. "Armando Renfield once served as the renfield to Dracula's council of vampires, making him the second highest ranked renfield in Transylvania when it fell. Since Dracula's personal renfield had no surviving family, and I am Armando Renfield's blood descendent, that makes me the highest–ranking member of this church short of a vampire. Which means by the Books of Blood, my word is *law*. White, you are about to lose rank as you are forcing me to ask my question a second time."

Deacon White groveled, bent at the waist and staring intently at the floor. "I'm sorry, Private Jonas."

"Lord Renfield will do."

"Yes, Lord Renfield. Count Bishop Rutter is presiding over a service."

"This is not a holy day of obligation. There was no service scheduled," Private Jonas said.

Deacon White's shoulders hunched and he put his palms up as he moved his hands out to his sides apologetically. "True, but the Count Bishop felt it best…"

"To make sure there would be no one but you to greet me, compounding his insult even more. Bring me to the worship grounds."

"But Lord Renfield, once begun, a Sangre service is not to be interrupted."

"And if there hadn't been a grave insult to the only renfield on this world, it wouldn't be. Take me there."

"As you command, Lord Renfield."

Deacon White shuffled off, motioning for Private Jonas to follow. After a long trek through a few hallways and three locked doors, they came to a great foyer with huge great doors that led to the church building proper.

In front of the doors stood two large gentlemen. The one on the left was six foot seven and the one on the right was at least 2 inches taller.

As Private Jonas stepped towards the door, the taller of the two men in white robes stepped forward and wrapped his fingers around the front of the sapper's uniform.

Private Jonas was all too aware that he would never win a fair fight with this giant but he was a soldier. Any soldier who survived his first battle knows you never want to be involved in a fair fight if you can help it.

With his right hand, Jonas grabbed hold of the giant's pinky then bent and twisted it until he heard it pop. With his left, he pulled out a collapsible baton metal baton and shook it to its full length, then used it to smash the giant's kneecap, shoulder, nose, and neck. The giant was used to getting by because he was stronger than everyone else and was caught off guard by the swift and brutal attack. Jonas kept swinging and hitting until the giant fell unconscious.

"This heretic dared to lay hands on a renfield!" Private Jonas shouted then turned and pointed his baton at the slightly smaller man in white robes. "And you stood by and allowed it to occur?"

The big man looked confused, then turned to see the deacon's head and shoulders bowed and realized something was wrong.

"We were only told that a member of the 142nd Starborne was coming. No one informed us that you were a renfield."

"Yet another thing that Rutter will answer for." Private Jonas looked down at the baton-battered giant, then back up at the big man. "Are you telling me that neither of you was informed of my imminent arrival?"

The big man shook his head frantically. "No, Renfield, sir."

"Lord Renfield," Deacon White corrected.

"Apologies, Lord Renfield. We were not."

"And is this poor fellow a good man and devout member of the church?"

The big man now enthusiastically bobbed his head up and down. "Yes, Lord Renfield. Very much so."

Private Jonas stroked his chin. "Then his actions were not heretical to the church, only ignorant. And does not King Dracula tell us in the Books of Blood that devotion and loyalty should be rewarded?"

The big man's head kept going up and down as if it had become a bouncing ball. "Yes, he does, Lord Renfield."

"Then this beating will serve as his only punishment. Take him and have him looked after."

Private Jonas moved towards the doors.

"Begging your pardon, Lord Renfield, but it is our job to make sure the service is not interrupted before the conclusion. It is against the commandments for you to enter," the big man said, his head and shoulders bowed in the same fashion as Deacon White's.

"If it was a valid service, you would be correct and I would honor your request. However, is it not also written that the highest ranking member of the Sangre Temple must be invited to any special services called by the clergy?"

The big man lifted his head and raised his eyebrows in obvious confusion as he didn't know the answer. He looked to Deacon White who nodded his head.

Relieved, the big man answered, "Yes, it is."

"As the direct blood descendent of Armando Renfield, am I not the highest-ranking member of the church on this world?"

Again the big man looked to Deacon White who repeated his nod.

"You are."

"And I was not invited. Therefore, this is a false blood service and I would see it end rather than continue with blasphemy. Now go take care of our brother in blood and see that he is cared for. I will include him in my prayers tonight."

"Yes, Lord Renfield."

Private Jonas couldn't believe that this was working and that the belief of the church members gave him this much power. Ricco realized he could learn to enjoy this.

Jonas forced away a smile as he put his hands on the double doors.

8

"Emissary, if you'll kindly wait here, the governor will be with you momentarily."

Tungsten knew immediately that the aide was lying as she was shuffled into the conference room, but she was above all a diplomat so she had much practice pretending to believe lies.

If she needed any confirmation of her suspicions, the click as the door closed behind the exiting aide would have done the job. Tungsten was far too well-trained to let her expressions or body language betray her inner thoughts. After all, she knew there were hidden cameras watching her. Her visor had a viewer that could "see" through walls. The emissary sat in the chair at the head of the conference table, her spine ramrod straight in a posture that would've been difficult to imitate by anything shy of a sculpture. She simply stared in front of her, focused on her breathing, and counted slowly to nine hundred. Fifteen minutes was the maximum reasonable time for one to pretend to believe an obvious lie.

Not bothering to try to open the door, she instead hit the speaker button to its left.

"A moment in medieval England was considered to be ninety seconds. I have given the governor ten times that out of courtesy. Unlock the door and take me to him immediately."

The voice of the aide who had led her into the room answered in a far less polite tone than he had used to her face. "The governor sends his regrets. We were told to show you all courtesy due a traitor to the Sway. Allowing you in the building is courtesy enough."

"You speak quite bravely for an underling addressing the highest-ranking member of the Sway he has ever met. If you will not let me out, I will do it myself."

The aide chuckled. "Nice bluff, Emissary."

The emissary allowed the hint of a smile. "You know that an

emissary's clearance is higher than that of the governor and I can override any Sway system."

"That would be true if the governor had allowed you to sign into the system so it recognized your credentials. He did no such thing so you have no more security clearance here than a laid-off factory worker."

"Foolish boy. Emissaries don't need to be signed into any system." That was an out-and-out lie. As expert as she was at pretending to believe lies, those skills were nothing compared to her ability to tell them. In the wee hours of the night, Major Benedict himself had led a team of sappers to get Tungsten into both the colony's main Sway security system and that of the governor's mansion to enter her credentials, all without alerting either the governor or his police force. Once in, she used her clearance to erase any trace of having signed in as well as ensuring that both she and Major Benedict had overrides on all the Sway systems.

"We both know that that's either delusion or a fairytale. Sit down and be quiet. If you're good, I'll bring you some food in about three hours."

"How very kind of you. If you don't mind me asking, which office is yours?" The visor showed several heat signatures in the surrounding rooms. "The tiny little one in the middle?"

"You're trying to diminish my importance isn't going to phase me, Emissary. Not that it could since I'm sitting at my desk in the large corner office. The one with the view."

"Thank you for that. System, lock office 15 Delta–" Benedict had had her memorize building plans so she would have the tools to use the system to her advantage. "–and unlock this door."

Emissary Tungsten pushed the door open and allowed herself a proper smile as she heard the aide banging on the locked door to his office. The system lock also disabled his communication systems.

Tungsten spoke into her wrist communicator. "System, lock and secure all hallways, rooms, and components between me and the governor. Disable all communications in the complex. And display a map of the route." A hologram flashed into being on her visor. After giving the system a few more orders, she moved to follow the illuminated path until she reached the secure door of the governor's office.

"System, unlock this door."

There was a small click as the emissary pushed the door inward. The governor looked up, surprised to see her.

"I'm going to fire Cheney." Cardell pressed a green button on his desk. "Security, would you please come to my office and remove the emissary."

Surprised by the lack of response, the governor pressed the button again and repeated his order.

"That won't do you any good. Get up off your ass and make me a cup of tea if you can handle that. We have much to discuss."

9

"What you are planning will destroy the planetary economy," Sergeant Ajani Opara said.

"We have an opportunity to do something that no union has ever managed before. We can take control of the means of production for the common working man and woman," Granja Union President Taft said.

"But you are promising your members ownership and that they won't have to work anymore. That's simply not viable. Even if you manage to get the current rich to switch places, there aren't enough of them to work the farms or the factories. Figure in that those replacements don't have the skills to perform those jobs and it means people will starve and die. You could at least be honest and say that they'll have a share in ownership but they will have to continue to work."

The union boss shook his head. "That's just not enough motivation. Dangling a carrot in front of them is enough to get them to work but not to fight a war."

Opara sighed. "Why does there have to be a war?"

"When Earth went up in flames so did the Sway's entire economic network. With warships destroyed, there isn't enough to justify building weapons and without the regular schedule and shipping infrastructure, we haven't been able to sell our excess food off-world. Factories laid off ninety percent of our workers, the farms forty percent. The union had to physically step in to redistribute the food that normally would've been shipped off-world so that our members and their families could eat. That brought the cops down on our necks. We're not going to let our members starve when there is food rotting in the fields."

Sergeant Ajani Opara nodded. "Nor should you but this seems to be a lot of wiggle room between getting your members working again and going to war against your fellow citizens."

"The government has left us no choice. They could've

redistributed the food themselves. Instead, they tried to extort every last mark people had saved. The Sangre came in claiming to want to do the same thing we were but the food they took didn't go to anyone except those blood-drinking maniacs. If people wanted food, they'd give it *if* the hungry joined their church. The only way our union members are going to survive is if we control this world."

"The Granja controls this world? Or you control it?"

"The Granja. Of course, as long as I continue to have the support of the membership, I will lead the Granja, which is a win-win for everybody on Cameroon."

"Nothing would make me happier than a win for everyone. Question—when you got the food, you mention feeding your members and their families. Did you also make sure that everyone who was hungry got some, including families of government employees, the rich, and even members of the Sangre Temple?"

"The union's main responsibility is to take care of its own. Besides those others weren't hurting as badly as we were. I have no regrets. If I had to do it again, I would."

"Does that include when your members who took the food killed the ranch and farm security forces, not to mention several police?"

Taft shrugged. "Their actions were causing people to starve. Those lackeys to the governor could have stepped aside. They knew what they were doing when they went to work each day. I'd rather they all died rather than one innocent child."

"A compelling argument but I'm not sure I agree with it. Especially since there is plenty of evidence that you actually sold the food to your members."

"That's ridiculous. How would I sell things to people with no money?"

"The Sway did away with things called credit cards and interest-bearing loans. True, they owned everything, but anyone could buy a house and other things within their means. But since the union teaches about these ancient evils, you knew about them and decided to bring them back to your own people. You sold to union members on credit, something most of them have never heard of. They sold you their futures so they and their families could survive the present. You made the interest so high that by the time most of the members start working again, they'll owe so much money that most of their wages will go back to the union. To get food from the Sangre Temple, people just had to go to church. They could always quit later."

"Don't kid yourself. Those bloodsuckers wouldn't let anyone leave their church alive. I saved people!" Taft said.

"You weren't saving anybody. You brought back the ancient company store with you as the new boss, the same as the old boss."

The union president smiled and nodded, mistaking the reason for Ajani Opara's concern. "I hear what you're saying. Before Earth turned to ash, the home office of the Granja would've gotten their cut. Now that you're here, I recognize that you may be the home office's last living representative and I'll make sure you–" Taft leaned forward and put his hand to the side of his mouth to whisper, "–or the 142nd Starborne if you prefer, get your cut. In exchange, all we ask is that you simply help us against help us in our current–" The union president made air quotes using his index and middle fingers, "–negotiations."

"And if we prefer not to?" Opara said.

"Then we ask that you simply don't interfere with our side of the negotiations. Money is all well and good but it always pays to back a winner."

"In terms of ordnance, you seem well behind the others. According to our calculations, you only have two G-1 mechs left. Compared to your competitors with ten P-1s each. Plus, the governor has his police force, vehicles, and weapons which seems to put him in the most advantageous position."

"It may look that way, but as a union man you know damn well not to show all the cards in your hand at the start of any negotiations."

"So you're saying you're better armed than the governor's police force? Civilians are not permitted to have guns." Sergeant Ajani Opara said.

"While you may be in the Granja, you're also in the 142nd Starborne so I absolutely am not saying we have guns. Then again, I'm not saying that we don't. Something else for you to consider– there are more weapons than just guns and mechs. All I'm saying is that if you want to back a winner, you should always go union. Besides, even if I am charging, I'm feeding more people than either of the other two. People are better off with me in charge."

10

"Major Benedict, we've picked up something on our sensor probes."

"What is it, Lieutenant Ghazali?"

"It appears to be a long-range intersystem freighter. I suspect it is likely a smuggler judging by the way it's trying to keep itself between the planet and its second moon. Its path is designed so planetary sensors would have a devil of a time noticing it. They did not plan for our sensor probes."

"I assume you've already initiated smuggler protocols?" Major Benedict said.

"Yes, sir. Just confirming with you that you want to keep them in place," Lieutenant Hamza Ghazali said.

"I do, particularly since the most valuable thing on Cameroon to smuggle out would be our missing mechs and drones. Maybe we can use these smugglers to find them. Do our new friends have any idea we are here?"

"They don't seem to. Of course, we are using the same trick in reverse, keeping our orbit near the planetside of a moon to stay hidden from anyone entering the system. The freighter is broadcasting an encrypted message to the planet. Our jammers are ensuring it doesn't reach the surface and is also making sure that no one from the planet can communicate with them," Lieutenant Ghazali said.

"Sir, using the incoming message's encryption as a guide, I am scanning communications leaving the planet and have picked up one with similar encryption," Lieutenant Nari Yun said.

"Have you broken the encryption yet so we know what they're saying to each other?"

"Not yet, sir, but it shouldn't be long. It looks like they're using a modified version of the Turning IV code. I should have it figured out in moments," Lieutenant Yun said.

"While we're waiting, launch six furies and have them hide

behind the moon until the freighters are inside the intercept perimeter."

The major's orders were relayed to the fighter bay and a half dozen Furies were launched in just over three minutes.

"I've got it, sir. Message from the surface reads *Awaiting pickup at your earliest convenience. Be aware, Behemoth is in orbit.* The one from the freighter reads *We will be arriving shortly.* Nothing incriminating in either one," Lieutenant Yun said.

"Yet not exactly aboveboard either with that warning about us. Where's the message planet side coming originating?"

"A little over 15 kilometers northwest of Depot."

"Send four drop ships with a full contingent of troops on each. Have them stay out of sensor range and deploy stealth drones. In the meantime, send the planetside message to the freighter but edit out the bit about us being here."

"Sir, the freighter has responded with an ETA and that they have the requested merchandise."

"I'd say that's enough reason for a surprise inspection. Is the freighter inside the intercept perimeter?"

"It will be in under three minutes."

"Then in three minutes and one second, message the furies to engage and immobilize that freighter for an inspection."

One hundred and eighty-one seconds later, the holographic display on *Behemoth's* bridge showed the freighter joined by matching light versions of the half dozen furies fighters. The freighter attempted evasive maneuvers and was met with a half dozen warning shots across various parts of her hull.

The freighter was outmatched and outgunned. The smart move would have been to power down and surrender. Instead, they went with choice B. The freighter jettisoned four panels, one on the top, bottom, starboard, and port sides of the ship–at least as much as such designations matter without gravity–revealing military-grade energy cannons.

The freighter fired at the furies, managing to hit one.

"Artemis Gamma Four, fall back. Everyone else, target to disable their weapons but leave the ship intact," Major Hamish

Kogan ordered from the lead fury fighter in Artemis squad.

Forward gunners on each fury took aim and fired upon the freighter with energy cannons of their own. Direct hits to the port cannon slagged it and near misses to the lower cannon knocked out its power supply.

The five intact furies moved out of the targeting range of the pair of remaining cannons.

"Freighter, this is Major Kogan of the 142nd Starborne. This is your second and final warning. You are hereby ordered to power down your drive and remaining other weapons."

The starboard cannon began to swivel and the front, side, and rear gunners on the furies opened fire, destroying the cannon and part of the hull.

"One more shot to your starboard cannon will result in a hull breach. We will fire again in one minute if you are still powered up or your remaining weapons read as hot," Major Kogan said.

The ship and weapons were powered down before the fifty-second mark.

"Freighter, your ship will be boarded for inspection. Attacks on any member of the 142nd Starborne will be met with deadly force. Acknowledge."

"This is Captain Fraser of the Atlas class freighter *Fardell*. Message is acknowledged."

11

ount Bishop Rutter stood in his deep crimson robes on a high altar in front of the congregation. In the center of the altar, there was a raised wooden coffin in front of which he marched dramatically.

"Are we not obligated by what is written in the Books of Blood to do as our Lord and Savior Dracula has commanded us and…"

The sermon was interrupted by a pair of wooden doors slamming hard into the walls.

The entire congregation turned in shock to watch Private Ricco Jonas stride in as if the church was a battlefield he had just taken by force.

"How dare you," Count Bishop Rutter bellowed, "interrupt our scared service!"

Private Jonas pointed his finger at the Count Bishop as if it were a sniper rifle ready to pick him off. "How dare *you* defy the Commandments of Blood to commit blasphemy in front of this congregation!"

Private Jonas kept marching towards the altar so Count Bishop Rutter rushed down to intercept him.

"You have no right to even be present!" Rutter yelled.

"By the books of blood, I have all rights. By not inviting me here you have blasphemed!"

"I cannot blaspheme against some soldier tool of the Sway."

Private Ricco Jonas stepped around the Count Bishop and rushed up onto the altar towards a marble font that lay beneath a metal spike.

Rather than prick his finger on the spike, Private Jonas pulled a knife from his waistband and pricked his finger. Holding it over the marble font, the sapper squeezed three drops of blood into the center onto a golden sensor. An instant later the machinery within the font had tested his blood. Crimson lights flashed around the altar.

Private Jonas held his bloody finger up in the air. "As our Lord Dracula has said, blood does not lie. I am Ricco Jonas, direct blood descendent of Alfonso Renfield, the renfield to Dracula and the Vampire Council of Transylvania. I was not invited to this service which means Rutter has blasphemed!"

The most devout of the congregation threw themselves forward from their pews onto their knees and bowed until their hands and faces touched the floor. Other members of the church, perhaps not so devout looked around awkwardly and slowly did the same until finally all members of the congregation were in that position except for the Count Bishop.

"Benedict never said anything about you being a renfield," Rutter said. "Had I known, I certainly would've made other arrangements."

"Did I ask to hear excuses? Why are you still standing in my presence?" Rutter glared at Private Jonas with the distilled essence of purest hatred burning in his eyes. "Do you think yourself the better of a renfield? Do you think the Commandments of Blood do not apply to you, Count Bishop?"

"Of course not. I am Dracula's most loyal servant."

"Then why are you still standing?"

Turning his body so his fury was hidden from his congregation, Count Bishop Rutter slowly bent down to subjugate himself on the floor.

Private Ricco Jonas turned and walked to the chair that stood behind the coffin altar. It was not so much a chair as it was a throne, made to resemble that of King Dracula. It is where Count Bishop Rutter typically sat.

Private Jonas planted his posterior onto the extremely comfortable cushion and placed his elbows on the armrest. "Start over from the beginning and this time, let's do it right."

He did his best to ignore the ritual bloodletting and drinking.

12

"You're insane. I'm the planetary governor. My word is law."

"Incorrect. The Sway's word *was* law. You were just their mouthpiece. If you had any leadership skills, you wouldn't be facing a revolution on two fronts. You have little choice in the matter. You will do what I say. Unlike some of the other colony worlds we've encountered since the conflagration, you stayed on the Sway mark where other worlds transitioned to their own forms of currency. I can shut down your entire planet's banking system. In fact, I've already shut down your account and that of your office."

"I don't believe you."

"Whether or not you believe will not change what is. See for yourself. System, unlock Governor Cardell's system interface."

The governor first used the holograph system and then the backup touchscreen.

"My personal funds are frozen and I can't get into any of my office accounts."

Emissary Tungsten nodded sagely. "See how ineffectual false belief is against a harsh reality. Your office will default on payroll for all employees including your police force. I wonder how this will be interpreted by people whom you are asking to fight and die for you. Tomorrow is payday too, isn't it? I wonder what will happen once your employees learn they're not going to be paid. I imagine there will be much resentment and unhappiness, don't you? I'm sure a man of your depth and skills will figure out a solution."

"How exactly am I supposed to do that? Offer them office supplies?"

Emissary Tungsten nodded. "That is one of the drawbacks of digital currency. From the governing point of view, it makes it very difficult to conceal funds when there's no physical representation of money. Luckily, I and the 142nd Starborne are willing to step in to make sure you can meet payroll although it will come with conditions."

"I will not leave office quietly," Cardell said.

"I have no interest in taking over your office. At least for the moment. My intentions are simple. I am here to make sure the citizens of Cameroon are safe, protected, and can live their lives without fear of dying in a crossfire."

"So you'll back me against the Sangre and the Granja?"

"That remains to be seen. Thus far you have not inspired any confidence in your ability to govern fairly. Then again neither have your two rivals."

"Have you shut down their accounts as well?"

Emissary Tungsten nodded. "And I can shut down the entire colony's access to money and turn your planetary recession into a depression. However, I am against that option unless my hand is forced. Now explain to me how, with warehouses food of preserved food that could not be shipped off-world, a large portion of your citizens are going hungry."

13

"Fury Team Gamma's mission was successful. Ninety–two crew members and the freighter were captured. No casualties on either side but Fury Gamma Four sustained damage as did the captured Atlas freighter," Colonel Bai Zhang said.

"Did they share what they were doing in the system?" Major Hans Benedict said.

"While they were cooperative with their boarding and capture all they were not so cooperative in answering any of our questions," Captain Shana Morales said.

Major Benedict sighed and nodded.

"This puts us at a crossroads," Colonel Zhang said. "Host protocol states that if prisoners are not forthcoming on initial questioning, corporal measures may be employed to gather needed information."

"I don't think any of us are comfortable using out-and-out torture to gather information. We've all had issues when a superior or commanding officer employed those techniques without a damn good justification. I don't see any clear and present danger. There is nothing they can tell us that can prevent the loss of life or destruction of property." Benedict said.

"I agree. However, that doesn't prevent us from presenting the illusion that the interrogatee will be harmed if we don't get the answers we want," Colonel Zhang said. "A large number of the crew are listed in our database as soldiers of the Host who are still on active duty. Which likely explains their reluctance to answer questions as the Host has used punishment up to and including a firing squad to punish deserters in the past. That they are here signifies either they abandoned their posts or we have a rogue element of the Host in play. As that could be dangerous for any world they come across, I personally would like to know which is the case. Especially since it appears that they were en route to pick up some heavy ordnance which could allow them to ransack any number of colony worlds."

"What are you suggesting?" Benedict said.

Shanna Morales smiled. "We start by giving some members of the 142nd a chance to show off any hidden acting abilities they may have."

14

Captain Fraser shuffled his way along the corridor with his ankles and wrists shackled together and a chain connecting the two so that he couldn't stand up straight no matter how hard he tried. Ahead of him, a guard opened an airlock door. Inside the airlock, someone wearing a brown freighter crew uniform lay bloodied and battered on a stretcher. The injured man was rolled out and down the corridor in the opposite direction. To the captured freighter captain, it looked as though he had witnessed the aftermath of the questioning of one of his crew when in reality he saw a member of the 142nd Starborne in makeup playing a part.

"Stand there," ordered the soldier escorting him. Fraser stood behind his lead navigator.

"What the hell happened to him?" Fraser whispered.

"The soldiers took him into the airlock for interrogation. All I heard was screaming then they brought Mann out on that gurney."

"That was Mann? I didn't even recognize him."

"Yeah, they worked him over pretty bad."

Colonel Zhang stepped out of the airlock dressed in a long white jumpsuit, covered in red dots and splotches. "You're next, former Lieutenant Eugene Burlingham. Before we begin you should know that there are two ways this questioning can go — painless or painful. Which one is up to you because you only get one chance to choose the former. What was the purpose of this freighter being in the Cameroon system and why was it crewed by AWOL Host soldiers?"

The freighter's navigator spit. Globs hit Zhang's chest and face.

"Go to hell, Colonel!"

"Very likely, but you'll get there before me, Burlingham, especially if you keep being this stupid. Not only did you reject the painless option but your pointless assault on my person has left me with no reason or desire to let you live. Let's begin."

Zhang snapped his fingers and two 142nd Starborne soldiers marched to either side of Burlingham, grabbed him by the elbows, then dragged him inside the airlock.

The airlock slid closed with a hiss. The freighter captain watched through the small airlock window as Burlingham was strapped to a gurney then disappeared from sight. Zhang's back was to Cameroon. The colonel shook his head as if he didn't like whatever answer he was given.

Zhang picked up a circular saw used to cut through metal and conduit for shipboard repairs and brought it down in front of him.

Crimson rain and hail spun through the airlock, joined by the thunder of pain and screams.

The soldier guarding Fraser noticed where his gaze was. "Eyes front, prisoner. You'll get a chance to see what's in there soon enough."

Fraser snapped his head forward but still strained to see through this tiny window out of the corner of his eye. He couldn't make out much other than more crimson rain and hail.

After what seemed like an eternity the heavy metal door hissed back open. Zhang and the two soldiers stepped out.

"No! Please, don't! I have a family," screamed the man on the gurney, his words punctuated by gurgling.

"We are better off without the likes of you. Shut the doors and vent the airlock," Zhang said.

"No! He didn't do anything to be killed for!" Fraser pleaded.

"I disagree. He, you, and the rest of your crew are listed as active duty soldiers of the Host in the 203rd Starborne. For you to be here means you've broken your oath and abandoned your post. That's treason, which in times of war is punishable by death," Zhang said.

"Who are we at war with?"

"That's classified. But it's obvious you were here to pick up the completed heavy ordnance that has yet to be commissioned.

That means you are a threat, which means you're on the wrong side of this war," Zhang said.

"What war?"

"What part of classified confuses you?" Zhang turned to one of the soldiers and nodded. The soldier turned a key and pressed a button. The space side airlock opened to the sound of a feeble scream that became fainter before ceasing altogether. The soldier pushed the button again and the outer airlock shut and sealed.

"We'll give it a moment to re-pressurize and then it will be your turn," Zhang said, pausing to flick a meaty chunk off his shoulder.

"Wait a second. You didn't give me a chance at the painless option," Fraser said.

Zhang shrugged. "I don't see a reason to bother. None of the other dozen we've questioned so far choose to take it."

"I would. I'm still loyal to the Host. I was in charge so I know more than anybody else."

Zhang's eyebrows raised. "What you have to say better impress me, Fraser."

"It will but I have one demand."

"We don't negotiate with deserters or traitors," Zhang said.

"Pretty shortsighted considering a lot of people are saying the 142nd Starborne committed mutiny and betrayed the Sway." Fraser put up his hands. "Not me, of course. Hear me out. I'll tell you what you want to know but, in exchange, you give me both your and the 142nd Starborne's guarantee that no more members of my crew will be tortured or killed. If you don't agree to that simple term, you might as well just put me out the airlock right now."

"Excuse me a moment." Zhang walked down the corridor then whispered into his earpiece. Zhang nodded and returned to stand opposite the prisoner.

"We agree to your term provided the information you give us is truthful, valuable, and you don't hold anything back."

Fraser nodded, figuring that was the best deal he was going

to get. "Obviously, you know we were in the system to take delivery of fifty X-1 mechs and a number of fighter drones."

"For what purpose? Redundancies built into the circuitry assure the weapon systems will self-destruct if you try to override them without the proper code too many times. All you'll have is scrap metal."

"The last time the 203rd Starborne received a delivery of X-1s, I managed to retrieve a video of the activation. It shows the entire activation code being entered by the Inspector General," Fraser said. "I mentioned that to a few crewmates and we all decided it was time for us to go into business for ourselves."

"You have the entire code?"

"Most of it. We are missing one digit but we have three tries to guess it before the self–destruct initiates. Since the missing code can be a letter or number, that means even if we guess wrong every time until the last try we would only lose nine of the mechs."

"Where is this recording?"

"On my personal tablet with the highest encryption available. I'm the only one who knows the passcode," Cardell said.

"What were your plans for having all that firepower at your disposal?" Zhang said.

"Find a decent size colony world like Rocky Top, take over, and set ourselves up as the rulers of the place. With that much ordnance, no one would be able to stand against us."

"Of course, you'd have to be able to keep mech pilots in line or worry about them all vying for the top position, but all in all, not the worst plan for taking over a colony that I've ever heard. Are you aware that there are over twenty stolen mechs that were not included in your sale?"

Fraser shrugged. "I knew we weren't getting it all. Part of the price we were paying was the activation code and if they wanted that it was because they had some mechs of their own they wanted to use."

"What was the rest of the price?" Zhang said.

"A few dozen military-grade rifles and ammunition.

Military-grade communication gear. And the fusion reactor pod from a Titan class cruiser."

Zhang furled his brows. "You have a Titan reactor pod in your possession?"

"We do."

"I take back what I said about your plan being half decent."

"What are you talking about? We're former soldiers, not monsters. We wouldn't threaten to blow up a city with the reactor or something like that," Fraser said.

Zhang rolled his eyes. "With that reactor, you'd be able to provide power to the largest city of any colony for nearly a century."

"Why would we give away free energy?"

"You wouldn't but you could have sold it. There are colonies out there that haven't had their power grids set up yet. You and your entire crew would have been set up for life with a guaranteed income without having to make a single threat or use a weapon. Wealthy without having any worries about trying to run a city or a colony. By the time the pod ran out of fuel, your entire crew and most of their children would likely be dead. Plus, you stole your freighter. Colonies are desperate to buy and sell with other colonies. For that to happen, the goods need to be transported. You could all have made a decent and honest living by transporting goods. Instead of using your brain, you came up with a convoluted scheme to set yourself up as a warlord. Warlords tend to kill people who resist them. Instead of taking one of two perfectly peaceful options available, you decided to kill people for personal gain. And give the code to other people who would use the ordnance to kill other people here on Cameroon."

Fraser shrugged and grinned sheepishly. "Hindsight, huh?"

"I'm going to need to see that recording," Zhang said.

Fraser tried to cross his arms over his chest but found that the shackles would not allow the movement. Instead, he grinned. "Then I'm going to need an addendum to our deal."

Zhang chuckled. "I'll keep that in mind. I gave you a choice to earn some goodwill and you just tossed it away. We have the

Fardell which means we have your tablet."

"That tablet has the highest level of encryption, remember? You will still need my passcode."

Zhang laughed. "Intent on proving your lack of intelligence once again, are you?"

Fraser's smile and confidence faded. "What do you mean?"

"Would that be top-level military encryption from your time in the 203rd Starborne perhaps?"

The freighter captain frowned.

"You think we won't able to break Host encryption? The same encryption we use every day?"

Zhang turned to the soldier who brought the captured freighter captain to his interrogation. "Return Mr. Fraser to his cell."

After the prisoner had been marched back down the corridor he'd come from and was out of sight, Zhang nodded to the soldier who had pushed the airlock button. He spoke into his earpiece and another pair of soldiers came out of the airlock with Mann and the freighter navigator in tow.

"Why did you put us in that safe box with these two? What was all that screaming? You never even asked me any questions," the freighter navigator said.

"Fortunately, I didn't need to. Thank you both for your cooperation," Zhang said.

15

"Captain Fraser, you have been cleared for landing," said the soldier pretending to be a freighter pilot, getting into character and addressing Major Benedict by the name of the man he was impersonating.

Benedict had not only been disguised to look like Fraser, he had been watching videos of him taken while his ship was being seized and of his interrogation. Sappers always did their best to imitate someone's physical mannerisms and voice.

The disguised Benedict nodded. "Put them in lights." Slang for putting them on the holographic viewer.

A man with a mop of blonde hair parted to the side above a shaved scalp smiled and lifted his hand in greeting.

"Captain Fraser, so glad could make it. Did you have any difficulty getting by the 142nd?"

"It was tough, Mr. Tark, but we managed it thanks to your warning. We left a beacon far out in the system and triggered it with a fake distress call. We ran silent near the moon until they took off to investigate the beacon. I don't think they're going to be gone long but certainly it's going to be a lot harder for us to leave so I'd appreciate if we can get through this as quickly as possible," Benedict said.

"Of course. Being a simple merchant, the last thing I want to do is have to worry about dealing with the 142nd Starborne. You're cleared for landing. See when you get here."

16

Jonathan Tark sent three communications, each with a different encryption but with the same message.

The Behemoth has left orbit but will return soon. If you're going to make your move on the power plant so you can control the entire colony, it's now or never.

Tark smiled thinking about how the three idiots would destroy each other's forces. With any luck, the power plant would be collateral damage from their fight. No reason to get involved more than just as a puppet master. Best to wait out the 142nd Starborne and let them chase after the three idiots who were fighting over control of the colony. Once the outsiders were gone, he could step in, set up his own power plant with the Titan reactor pod and then move from merchant and secret arms dealer to planetary ruler.

רו

In the union hall, President Taft stepped into the main conference room. Despite it being the middle of the night, the room was full, even if the men and women there were asleep on chairs and couches.

"Wake up! One of our supporters just let us know the *Behemoth* has left orbit but they weren't sure for how long. Now is our time to take control of the power plant. If we control that, we control Depot. If we control the capital then we control Cameroon. Assemble the members and get our forces ready to march."

"What about Opara?"

"It's too dangerous to risk trusting him. We don't know where his true loyalties lie–with the union or the 142nd. He should be asleep now in his bunk. The three of you go make sure he doesn't wake up ever again."

The three members strode out of the conference room.

Back in his tiny room, Ajani Opara pulled on his boots and a black jacket and tucked a shoe that was missing a heel into his front pocket. The night before he had arrived at Granja Union HQ, Opara snuck in with a sapper squad led by Captain Leon Juma as they bugged crucial areas in the union complex, including the president's office and the conference room. He received a beep in his embedded communicator whenever any noises were picked up.

Opara used pillows, blankets, and some clothes to make it appear he was under the covers. Then he crept out of his room and towards the nearest nontraditional exit, a third-story window. Opara fastened a grappling hook with a micro line onto the windowsill. The other end was attached to a reel in his belt buckle. Opara repelled down to the ground and removed the broken shoe from his coat. He squeezed the tip of the tongue and counted to ten, detonating the Z–5 explosives hidden in the right hip joints of both the homemade G-1 mechs. The explosives had originally been the heels on his shoes, a perfectly safe way to transport the material as it took an electrical current to detonate. The detonators had been disguised as the aglets of his shoelaces.

The duel explosions shook the building which he hoped would provide him cover as he ran onto the streets of Depot.

18

Private Ricco Jonas had never been so tempted to abuse power in his entire life as when he was facing three scantily clad nubile and obviously devout members of the Sangre Temple. He even turned his embedded communicator to standby so he wouldn't be teased mercilessly when he returned to *Behemoth* for not taking advantage of his current situation.

"I'm flattered, ladies. More than you can possibly imagine but it would be wrong for me to take you up on your amazing offer." The three women were of different heritages and hair colors.

The Amazon-sized redhead in the front who said her family originated in Scotland stepped forward and crossed her arms over her stomach. "Why, Lord Renfield? Don't you find us attractive?"

The woman stood three inches taller than Jonas did and he had to make a conscious effort to look up at her eyes rather than down into her cleavage. "Trust me, it's not that. All of you are very attractive women."

To his left, a woman with curly black hair whose family originated from Kenya said, "Maybe you prefer the company of men?"

Jonas shook his head and stepped back as she ran her fingers up his chest. "Definitely not."

The tiny woman to his right with blond hair whose family came from Thailand looked up at him and nibbled on the tip of her index finger. "Are you already married?"

Jonas shook his head. "No. I'm divorced."

The large woman in the center said, "Then why won't you celebrate the Festival of the Brides with us?"

Jonas's briefing had covered the major religious holidays of the Sangre, of which the Festival of the Brides seemed by far the most enjoyable, at least for the three highest-ranking members of any individual church. They got to choose three women from the congregation to act as their brides from sunset to sunset.

Other members of the church could celebrate but had to make arrangements on their own. However, he was certain the holiday wasn't due to be celebrated for several months. Jonas was even more certain that if it had been during the time he was inserted into the temple that he would have made a billboard-sized mental note of it.

"Because it would be wrong of me to use my position to coerce the three of you to have sex with me."

"You aren't making us do anything," said the tiny blonde. "You didn't ask us. We asked you. We find you incredibly sexy and we do this of our own free will."

"I'm not exactly looking for one wife let alone three," Jonas said.

Two of the women giggled. The amazon tittered. The one with the black hair said, "Who said anything about being a wife? This is about honoring the brides of our Lord and Savior Dracula. It's the time when the congregation gets to embrace the darker side of their sensuality. You wouldn't want to take that away from us, would you?"

"I wouldn't want to be considered a cad…" Jonas stammered as the woman stroked his arm. "But this isn't the right time of year for the Festival."

"The Count Bishop gets to pick two extra days to celebrate, one for each bride." The petite blonde stroked his other arm. "And if you turn us down, the Count Bishop has already chosen his brides so the third highest ranking member is Deacon White. The deacon is not sexy or attractive and he has said he will choose us as his brides."

"You could just tell him no," Jonas said.

"But we would lose our ranking in the congregation, so we really have no choice," the amazon said.

"You wouldn't want to make us have sex with Deacon White, would you?" the blonde asked.

Jonas tilted his head to the side. "Well, I certainly wouldn't want to have sex with Deacon White."

The redheaded Amazon reached her hand behind Jonas's neck and stepped in so her lips loomed a half-inch above Jonas's. "Then it's decided. For the remainder of the festival, we are your brides to do with as you will. We will obey your every command, Lord Renfield, and we offer this to you of our own free will."

"Our own free will," the other two echoed.

The amazon ran the tip of her tongue around the outside of her lips. "What would you have us do?"

Private Ricco Jonas leaned up to passionately kiss the amazon, then each of the other women.

His requests were unspoken but understood by the brides.

Sometime later, after being treated to the time of his life, Jonas rolled over onto his back onto the crowded bed in his quarters.

"Give me a moment to hydrate and catch my breath," Jonas said.

"Private Jonas, you are in grave danger," came a voice from his embedded communicator. Since it worked by vibrating his mastoid process, nobody else could hear the woman. "This is Lieutenant Nari Yun and I had to initiate an emergency override of communication standby. You are not supposed to do that in the field. All three factions are moving against the power plant. Get out of the Temple immediately and go to ground. We will send a pick up for you."

Jonas shot up. "What!?"

The blonde fell over his legs and wrapped her arms around them while the woman with the black hair pinned his arms with her body. From behind him, the amazon pulled a soaked cloth out of a sealed container and covered Jonas's mouth and nose with it.

"Sweet dreams, Lord Renfield," the amazon whispered as darkness claimed the soldier.

19

Emissary Sarah Tungsten saw the incoming message even before the governor did but could not break the encryption. Sometime after, the governor yelled for the police to start mobilizing. Tungsten didn't know why but his excitement was enough for her to whisper into her wrist controller and lock down the governor's complex.

The governor tried to leave his office and found his way locked, but this time he wasn't taken by surprise. Knowing that the emissary could monitor any communications through electronic systems, he'd taken to using paper notes and hand radios that were used as children's toys and broadcast, "Victory protocol alpha–1."

In the corridors leading to the emissary's suite, government employees removed pre–loosened panels and pulled power conduits free from their connections, then pressed the power switches to self–powered jamming devices that had been hidden inside the walls.

While the governor couldn't undo the lockdown order, he had effectively isolated and locked the emissary in her own rooms, unable to communicate with the greater system. An employee soon disconnected the power to Cardell's office and used a charged door jumper on the manual override that was hidden behind a panel that had been loosened in advance.

Knowing that the jammers might weaken the toy radios' signal, the go code made sure that all the governor's people moved to the vehicle garage where they would don body armor, receive weapons, and mobilize the remaining police mechs.

Since the emissary could shut down the communication and financial hubs for the colony at any time, there was only one target left that would give him control over the people.

Once his police force controlled the power plant there could be no challengers to his rule. He even shared his idea with his most ardent supporter and patron, Jonathan Tark, who thought it was brilliant. And as the third richest person on the planet, he valued the merchant's insight.

Even when the 142nd returned, they wouldn't be able to take back the power plant without destroying it. Since Benedict and his ilk seem to care more about the well–being of people than winning a battle, Governor Cardell knew they wouldn't risk that or damaging the colony's power supply, especially as that would leave hospitals in the dark.

Now, he even had the emissary as a hostage and could just kill her if Benedict tried anything.

Cardell once again considered if he should take a new title. King perhaps? No, something better. He would be Emperor Cardell the Magnificent.

20

The freighter touched down outside the remote complex in an area surrounded by trees, still a decade away from being mature enough to be turned into lumber. Jonathan Tark, flanked by fifty men with military-grade rifles, stood waiting, his spine ramrod straight and his hands clasped behind his back.

The back end of the freighter lowered down to become a ramp. The disguised Hans Benedict stepped out with a contingent of ten soldiers wearing the brown uniforms of the freighter crew. All eleven marched down as Tark stepped forward.

"Captain Fraser, a pleasure to finally meet you in the flesh." Tark extended his right hand.

Benedict reached out and shook it. "It's a happy day for all of us, Mr. Tark."

"You have the Titan reactor pod?" Tark said.

"It wouldn't be a very good start to our relationship if I didn't bring what I said I would, now would it?" Benedict said.

"Not that I would ever doubt your word, but may I see it?"

"Of course. It's on board. It's a little large to casually move around. You may come on board to inspect."

"And here's where we run into our first bit of trouble. Trust is so easy for one to offer yet so hard for another to accept because in our hearts we all know a universal truth. In this great big galaxy of ours, there are so very few who can truly be considered trustworthy. While we may have common acquaintances neither one of us has any reason to think the other is truly worthy of our trust. After all, we are dealing with technology that will allow us to rule over others. How much more would either of us accomplish if we were able to keep all the ordnance and the pod?"

"What you say is true but there is such a thing as being too greedy. We no longer have a unified currency between worlds and the value of a Sway mark varies greatly depending upon each world's inflation. While we could easily sell the reactor pod anywhere, what we'd get in exchange for it might be several fortunes on one world and pennies on another. However, power of the kind we are trading for travels with you anywhere. You, Mr. Tark, obviously have a use for the reactor pod. And only a fool wouldn't keep some mechs for themselves and you do not strike me as a fool. That means you have use of the code we possess. Neither of us has to trust the other to realize that by working together we can both come out ahead. In the interest of that mutual benefit, it would be foolhardy of me to invite you onboard my ship to then do you harm."

"I agree but perhaps for not the same reasons as you." Tark lifted his right hand above his head and snapped his fingers. From either side of the complex, the ground shook as a pair of fully commissioned military-grade black X-1 mechs marched their way into view. "Let me assure you that if you do anything to screw me over, your ship will never reach orbit."

Benedict's initial reaction was to mask his reaction, then realized the person he was imitating wouldn't have that presence of mind. He allowed his face to show his very real shock. "If you can already activate the mechs, what do you need our code for?"

"During the last pickup before Earth burned, the Inspector General activated all the mechs before loading them for delivery. A hacker in my employ who also worked at the factory managed to get into the records and change the number of mechs ordered to two fewer than were made. Using what in ancient times was known as a shell game, I managed to get these two away after they were activated but before they were shipped, all without the Host being aware they existed, let alone were missing."

A flock of fighter drones took to the air. "As well as five drones. While being in control of this armament puts me in a well-protected position, it is simply not enough for my long–term plans. That is where you and your compatriots come in. In fact, I don't even have to go on board your ship to verify that you have what you say you do."

Tark pointed to the nearest drone and then to the open bay of the freighter. The drone flew in as a man came to stand in front of Tark holding a tablet. Benedict looked at the screen which showed an aerial view of the freighter Bay as it hovered over the reactor pod.

"Sensors show the reactor pod is at ninety–six percent of capacity," the lackey said.

Tark smiled and nodded once. "Verification is so much better than having to rely on trust, don't you agree?"

"As long as you're the one who can do the verifying, I suppose it is. Now if you don't mind returning the favor and showing us our X-1s."

"Don't get us ahead of yourself, Captain. They only become yours if your code turns out to be good. If it doesn't, I'm going to kill you and every last member of your crew for destroying the mechs I allow you to enter the code on."

As if to emphasize Tark's words, the two mechs marched to stand on either side of the group of men.

"Fair enough." The disguised Benedict put his hands behind his back and craned his neck to look up at mech, then the other. "Truly impressive feats of violence and engineering, aren't they?"

Tark nodded. "That they are."

"Mr. Tark, would you mind if I just touched each of them to get a feel for the power that will be in my control once our deal is successfully concluded."

Tark chuckled. "Power is intoxicating, isn't it? You may touch one then let's get on with this."

Benedict reached out so that the thimble he concealed under a glove pressed up against an external sensor port on the one mech's leg. The slight vibration it made on contact went unnoticed by everyone else.

There was a warehouse behind the main house where dozens upon dozens of mechs were lined up in the center of a cavernous room as if standing at attention. A greater number of drones lined the floor along the walls around them.

"As you can see, here's the merchandise as promised. Now show me your surveillance video and we'll get started."

"No," said Benedict.

Tark's eyes narrowed and his teeth ground together. "Excuse me?"

"You demonstrated that you have the upper hand in terms of firepower. Once I show you that video, you'll have no need to keep me or my people around any longer. I plan to live long enough to leave this world with my merchandise in tow. To make sure that happens, I will enter the code and my guess for the last digit solo. Once I have two activated mechs and five activated drones, I will share the code with you. At that point, if you decide to not honor our deal, at least it'll be a fair fight," Benedict said.

"I'm hardly thrilled at your lack of trust but I can respect it. What's to stop me from slaughtering your compatriots and torturing you give me the video?"

"Because the video doesn't exist anymore. I erased it,"

"You did what!? Did you at least write it down somewhere?"

Benedict put a finger to his temple. "It's all up here."

"The code is fifty characters long."

"We don't know the last digit so technically it's only forty-nine. However, that de-incentivizes you for torturing me. Any damage to my cranium might mean I might forget something crucial or juxtaposition a number. In addition to shooting all my people, it'll be putting a bullet in your own foot. Pity I just couldn't say–" Benedict lifted his hand to his chin and stroked it with his gloved thumb. "–Slave mech to my controller."

Benedict shrugged and took his hand away from his mouth. "But since that doesn't appear to be an option, we will simply have to trust each other for a little bit longer."

Tark stared at the man he thought was Captain Fraser to take stock of the man. Nodding, he said, "I guess we will."

Tark motioned to the black X-1 at the front of the line. Benedict walked to the one behind it and used his body and hands to provide cover as he popped open the control pad box. The box would do one of two things. If the code was entered correctly, it would activate the mech. If it was entered three times incorrectly it would issue the self-destruct message which would melt most of the mech's circuitry and weapons to slag. Either way, once either of those tasks was done, it would fall off.

Benedict entered the code once and nothing happened. The same thing happened the second time. He moved away from the mech.

"Why are you stopping?" Tark said.

"Why would I destroy my own merchandise? I will leave one good try on each mech. That way once I figure out the code, I can come back and enter it."

"That seems logical but that means if your code doesn't work, you're not leaving me many tries on what will end up staying my merchandise."

Benedict shrugged. "If they end up staying yours, you'll still have one shot at each instead of a pile of slag. Seems like a win for you too."

"Fine. Continue."

Benedict did. When he got to the seventeenth mech, the second code he entered worked but the box didn't fall off. That was part of the plan. When he opened each box, he slipped a razor-thin electromagnet between the box and the mech.

Benedict touched the interface on the box with the covered thimble, he slaved it to his control. Without that, any activated mech could be piloted by anyone.

"Silent mode," he whispered toward the thimble.

The X-1 made no overt sounds as Benedict moved to the next one.

"What was that?" Tark said.

"I said here we go," Benedict covered. "Only two more tries and we'll have it."

"You better pray for your sake that it works," Tark said.

"It will." Benedict twisted and straightened the back of his collar. That was the signal to the ten soldiers who'd come in with him that the previous X-1 was activated. One of them pressed a button on their sleeve which sent the signal to another soldier hidden in the freighter who sat in a remote pilot's seat. Benedict slipped the electromagnet between the box on the next mech, then turned to Tark. "You might as well come over here and watch because if this doesn't work the next one will."

Tark squinted at Benedict. "I thought you wanted two mechs and five drones activated before you gave me the code."

"If you can remember fifty digits in a row, more power to you," Benedict said, pretending he didn't know Tark had a micro camera hooked to his shirt collar.

Tark stepped forward as did his armed people, allowing three of Benedict's fellow sappers to slip away from the crowd and start entering the code on other ordnance. The sappers also had memorized the forty–nine digits and knew the sequence that Benedict was using to figure out the missing character. Each sapper activated two drones before moving on to mechs.

They caught the control boxes as they fell off, making sure the falling boxes didn't give them away then climbed inside the walking tanks.

Benedict had made a show of entering the code slowly and incorrectly. When he got to the fiftieth digit nothing happened. The last digit he entered was nine.

"You started with the alphabet first?" Tark said.

Benedict nodded.

"Which means the last digit is zero?"

It was the 22nd digit that was missing, not the last one, but Benedict nodded.

Tark pulled out his sidearm and pointed it at Benedict. "I guess I don't need you anymore. You should have checked me for cameras."

Benedict pointed in the air behind them at the six flying drones hovering overhead. "You should've kept a better eye on my people."

Three black X-1s marched off the line.

With Tark and his people distracted, Benedict ducked between the legs of the mech, sprinted to the back line of mechs and hurriedly entered the correct code in an X-1 before climbing into the pilot's seat.

In the meantime, the three sappers in X-1s had surrounded Tark's men. The first one activated was spun by its remote pilot and pointed its gun arm at Tark.

"Destroy the freighter!" Tark shouted into his collar microphone.

The sound of large cannons firing outside the warehouse was unmistakable.

"You may have us slightly outnumbered but my people have been practicing," Tark said. "My two mechs will beat your three and my five drones will beat your six."

"Actually, that cannon fire was one of your mechs taking down the other one," Benedict said through the mech's speakers.

Through the pilot's canopy, Benedict looked up at the six floating drones and nodded. Five flew out of the building.

"I feel comfortable saying that my drone pilots will blow your drone pilots out of the sky. While your people might've been practicing, mine have been trained and actually used drones in combat. Allow me to factually introduce myself. I am Major Hans Benedict of the 142nd Starborne and you are in our custody. Surrender or we will destroy you."

Tark and his people in the warehouse wisely placed their weapons down and surrendered.

One by one, Benedict and the other three sappers got out of their mechs and allowed other soldiers to take their places in the pilot seat. Each of the sappers moved to a new mech, activated it, and repeated the process until a majority of the soldiers hidden inside the freighter were piloting a mech. The sappers then went to work on activating the drones.

21

Private Ricco Jonas woke in a stone cell with iron bars.

The only light in his cell was a primitive battery-powered torch on the wall outside of his cell. He sat up with a start, realized he was still naked, and looked for something to cover himself with. He was the most junior sapper in the 142nd and his first thought was he was never going to live this down. His second thought was that at least he'd have the chance to live it down.

Outside the cell, Count Bishop Rutter sat in a chair with his legs crossed.

Rutter smiled. "You're awake. Did you enjoy my special Festival of the Brides?"

"Up until I was rendered unconscious, I had no complaints. What the hell's going on?"

"You've been unconscious for twenty minutes," Lieutenant Yun said through Jonas's embedded communicator. "What is your status?"

"Why am I in this cell?" Jonas said.

"Captured. Understood. We will send an evac squad as soon as one is available. Try not to die in the meantime," Yun said.

Not realizing Jonas was communicating with *Behemoth*, Rutter said, "You should be kinder. I could have just had one of the ushers knock you out from behind, except that those two giants believe you are a renfield and that would lead to some questions I would rather not answer. I just learned that the *Behemoth* left orbit–"

"Jonas, I can assure you we have not, but that is what Major Benedict planned to tell an arms dealer. The dealer must be in communication with Rutter. I will be monitoring you, but I need to check for communications leaving the arms dealer's complex. Holler if you need me," Lieutenant Yun said.

"–and I needed to get you out of the way. Even as we speak, the blood warriors of the Sangre Temple are marching on the city's power plant. A secret member of the congregation was kind enough to point out its value as a target." Rutter understood why Jonathan Tark kept his membership and true beliefs hidden. Many of the colony worlds would not want to do business with one of Dracula's chosen and the Sway would have canceled all his business licenses. However, the merchant was the Temple's most generous donor so his public cowardice could be excused. "Once we hold that, people won't want to give up their energy because not only will they have no entertainment, heat, or air conditioning, but their water will stop running as will their sewage. Not even the 142nd Starborne would risk destroying the power plant and thereby depriving all the people in the city of power. We will be triumphant."

"Why go to all this trouble? Why not just kill me?"

"Jonas, some advice. Don't look a gift horse in the mouth, especially if it has fangs," Lieutenant Yun said in his communicator.

Rutter put his upper leg down and then crossed the other. "Because there are those in the church to truly believe in the scriptures as written. If I were to be perceived in any way as being behind your death, the congregation would kill me, drain my blood on the altar, and feast on it. By putting you down here, I can prove that you're still alive and that you approve of my actions."

"If you want to impress the congregants, then why aren't you leading the battle?"

"I've found it's best to lead from the rear. After all, there's no way of assuring that either the governor's forces or the Granja won't try to stop us. It was a good investment for us to buy our P-1s from the secret member of our congregation after he liberated them from the police. True, it emptied the coffers of the Temple, but in the long run it will pay off when we rule Cameroon. Once I control the city's power, it won't matter what anyone else has to say."

"So you'll let me go?"

"Or perhaps offer you as a going away gift to the 142nd Starborne to get them to leave the system for good. Now if you'll excuse me I have to go supervise my troops."

"From the safety of the control terminal next to your office?"

Rutter stood. "Safe is the best place to be in any battle."

22

"**M**ajor Benedict, we need you back on board *Behemoth* immediately," Lieutenant Ghazali announced in Benedict's ear.

"What's happening, Lieutenant Ghazali?"

"It looks like you're not the only one using the cover of night to try to pull off a fast one. Tark sent coded messages to all three rebel factions. We know the one to Rutter was for the Sangre to take control of the power plant while *Behemoth* is away. Lieutenant Yun is working to decode the other two messages but we are working off the assumption that Tark sent the same message to the other two factions," Lieutenant Ghazali said.

"Why are we assuming?"

"The governor's headquarters has gone dark and the forces of all three factions are mobilizing," Ghazali said.

"Have you heard from our intermediaries?"

"Yes sir. Private Jonas is imprisoned in the temple. Sergeant Ajani Opara is on the run, and the governor appears to be using signal jammers so we can't make contact with Emissary Tungsten."

"Damn it. Depot was already a powder keg. Is Captain Morales on the Bridge?"

"Once you were successful in acquiring the ordnance, Colonel Zhang suggested she get a few hours of sleep. We have already summoned her and expect her momentarily."

"There's no time to waste. Lieutenant, I want a dropship with three extraction teams heading for our people now. Then scramble every available harpy with half a contingent of troops to extract citizens from the neighborhoods around the power plant. I want the other half of the harpies kept empty for evacuations. These morons are going to get a lot of people caught in the crossfire. Our primary mission is to protect and evacuate. We will not engage unless fired upon or to protect citizens. Morales may alter my orders as she sees fit once she arrives. I will mobilize a contingency of our new mechs and drones to help."

Over the open channel, Benedict heard Lieutenant Yun announce, "Captain on the bridge."

"Major, Captain Morales is here," Lieutenant Ghazali.

"Good. Let her know my orders, Lieutenant. I will get our people here armored up and moving toward the city. Benedict out."

23

Since the factory layoffs, there was no longer night shifts in the city of Depot. This left the dark streets practically empty.

The troops and ordnance from all three factions marched down the middle of those streets. If there had been other people, the shooting would likely have started immediately. After all, the people holding guns and other weapons were civilians, not trained soldiers. The emotions running through the rebels were a mixture of excitement and terror. It made them jumpy and ready to shoot anyone who was not one of them. Each of them was certain an attack might come at any moment from any direction.

The power plant had its own security force but they were only armed with chemical irritant sprays and shock sticks. They had nothing that would hold off a small group of armed attackers, let alone three large groups convinced of the righteousness of their cause and willing to shoot others in the name of that selfsame righteous cause.

Mob mentality ruled as all thoughts of morality were pushed to the rear of conscious thought as their minds concerned themselves with staying alive.

The Sangre were the first to arrive. The security guards at the front gate couldn't be blamed for fleeing at the sight of the crimson P-1s. Their fellow security guards were equally blameless for racing off in their wake.

Before the forces of the Church of Blood could reach the gate, three police drones arrived overhead, firing at the Sangre who held their stolen guns, causing them to scatter. The pilots of the five crimson mechs fired into the sky. The drones performed evasive maneuvers. Two of the three soared away unscathed. The third was caught in the crossfire and plummeted into a nearby house.

The home caught fire.

The Granja may not have had police-grade armaments, but they had access to a lot of other equipment and the knowhow to adapt it. A dozen crop duster drones arrived in the sky, releasing part of their payload on the fleeing armed congregants of the Church of Blood.

Police arrived in riot vehicles. The crop dusting chemicals were designed to kill insects and fungi. On their own, they would not have done much immediate damage other than irritating eyes and making it difficult to breathe. But having worked for years in fields where the chemicals were sprayed, the Granja used their knowhow to upgrade the agricultural drones. They had been outfitted with long wires that hung down and were connected to a battery. A push of a button by the remote pilots caused sparks to fly from the ends of the wires and the sparks turned the clouds into fireballs.

The result was more of a flash explosion than a flamethrower but it still knocked out windows in the police vehicles, forcing many of the officers and congregants to hit the ground screaming and rolling to extinguish the flames hungrily devouring their clothing and skin.

Ajani Opara may have sabotaged the two remaining homemade union G-1 mechs, but the Granja still had tractors, dump trucks, and other heavy equipment which raced into the battle for the power plant.

One dump truck rammed into the legs of one then another of the crimson P-1s, knocking them down, but even overturned with a damaged leg, one of the crimson mechs fired its arm gun at the underside of the dump truck like Judah Maccabee attacking the elephants. The crucial difference being that elephants didn't have fuel tanks. The resulting explosion took out the dump truck, trapping the driver in the cabin as it filled with smoke.

The screams of the children in the nearby burning house were ignored in favor of making sure the slaughter went on.

The police mechs arrived and started firing on the crimson mechs and the heavy equipment as well as any people not in a police uniform. The Granja countered this offensive with a bulldozer with a makeshift flamethrower strapped to the front propelling fuel mixed with aluminum soap. Their homemade napalm clung to the outsides of the police mechs, combatants, and nearby rows of nearby houses.

The night streets finally became crowded as people ran screaming from their burning homes into the streets looking for a safe place to run and not be met with bullets or homebrewed napalm.

Not one person on any of the three sides thought about trying to help those who weren't involved in the battle, although some were decent enough at least to not fire weapons directly at unarmed civilians. At least, not on purpose, but that's the thing about friendly fire. It doesn't care who gets in the way.

Around the back of the power plant, a team of Sangre cut through the wire fence and crept towards the entrance of the power plant. In the front, a dump truck with a plow rammed through the fencing. Off on the side, a flock of four drones each carried a police officer over the fence toward the plant entrance.

It was a mad scramble to be the first side inside. Police dropped to the ground as the drones moved to fire at the opposition. A dozen union members with homemade pneumatic rifles filed out of the back of the dump truck, firing metal pellets at everyone else.

A single member of the Church of Blood and a planetary police officer made it to the door. Each tried to shoot the other, but their guns were out of ammo so the crimson-clad congregant pulled a blade and the officer pulled a shock stick and the pair circled each other warily. The Sangre lunged blade first but the police officer had been trained to fight and parried, taking her knife. He then jabbed out with his much longer shock stick at the congregant's abdomen then sliced her jugular with her own blade. The woman fell to the ground gripping her throat, her last words in this universe coming out as a gurgle.

The victorious police officer had turned towards the door when the dump truck smashed into him, crushing his ribcage and most of his internal organs. The officer fell and the dump truck backed up to run over him and crush more bones beneath its wheels.

The dump truck spun around to crash into the doors of the power plant, tearing them off the hinges and leaving a large opening into the plant.

The driver leapt out of the cab only to be shot in the back by a planetary police officer being carried through the air by a drone. She made it into the plant with others hot on her heels.

She took up position around the first corner and opened fire on anything not wearing a police uniform who tried to come through the newly expanded doorway. She soon learned the cover the wall provided was deceptive, as the building materials made poor armor as bullets from stolen guns slammed into and around her body armor, dropping her in one meaty, bloody mess.

A police P-1 made the door gap wider and taller by stomping its way through then walked down the hall, destroying it since it was higher and wider than the hallway was designed to handle.

On the other side of the building, one of the crimson mechs smashed through the outer wall to make its way towards the center of the plant, also destroying the ceiling and the walls around it as joined the bloody race toward the center of the power plant.

A makeshift armor–plated small vehicle, called a mule because of all the lugging its unarmored version did around a farm, chose a different hall but made better time as it didn't have to destroy the building as it went.

Outside the fires spread and Depot began to burn.

24

Sergeant Ajani Opara may have escaped from union headquarters but he hadn't gotten far. Three motorcycles ignored the explosions that destroyed the G-1s to chase after him.

Surprisingly, they did not race off into the night. If they had, he would have been able to slip away. They knew enough to ride a grid pattern. Worse, they were not being clandestine in their search.

"Be on the lookout for an enemy of the Granja sent here to spy on us," announced one of the riders on speakers loud enough to wake the mostly sleeping working-class neighborhood that surrounded union headquarters. "He has been sent here to kill union members. He should be considered armed and dangerous. Please come out and help find this enemy of the worker."

Many people in their night clothes had answered the call and joined in the search, starting with their own property, and then joining the grid search on foot.

The three motorcycles stopped to confer in the middle of the street near where Opara had taken cover behind some refuse bins. The property near the bins had already been searched so he figured he had at least a few moments before he had to find a new hiding place.

Ajani Opara had been outfitted with personal surveillance equipment. His embedded communicator had been programed to pick up signals from the parabolic disc microphone hidden in the button of his left sleeve. By pointing it in the direction of the three union members, he could hear their conversation as well as if he had been standing next to them.

"I can't believe we haven't found this spy yet. He couldn't have had much of a head start on us. You don't think he's a sapper, do you?"

"Bah," said a man he recognized as Patterson. "Opara is no

sapper, just a sap. If we take the power plant, we win. We don't know how long we have until the 142nd gets back. We need to have the plant under our control before they return. If Opara manages to get a message to them, they might come back early. That means if you find him, you kill him. Got it?"

The two other men nodded and resumed riding the search grid while Patterson used his headset to answer an incoming message.

"No sir, we haven't found him yet, but we will. No one's got a vehicle in this part of town and public transportation is shut down this time of night. Ajani Opara is as good as dead."

Patterson might've cursed the irony of the next and last moment of his life as a razor-thin metal wire was wrapped around his throat and pulled back hard enough to slice through skin, muscles, and blood vessels. Opara wasn't a Sapper but that doesn't mean Benedict didn't outfit him with enough hidden weapons to pass as one.

Opara snatched the headset as Patterson collapsed gurgling and holding his throat.

"Hello Mr. President, I am overjoyed to inform you that the rumors of Ajani Opara being near death are greatly exaggerated. However, the Granja membership has been lessened by the very recent death of Mr. Patterson."

On the ground, Peterson was not quite dead and reached under his shirt for a hidden sidearm. Opara ground his boot onto Patterson's blood-covered forearm and took the gun from his waistband. It was a custom pneumatic pistol. It was well made. It looked like the union had been having its machinists working overtime and off the books. It had a compressed air cylinder that fired small metal pellets at high enough velocity that it would penetrate muscle and bone as well as any small caliber bullet. Because of the tiny ammunition, the weapon held fifty rounds. When it was time to reload, both the ammo and the cylinder would need to be replaced.

"Opara, get yourself back here. This isn't personal. We're all just working for the benefit of the union and its members. I know you get that. I know you are just like me and bleed union."

"I'm definitely pro-union but I can't say I approve of your administration, especially after you sent a hit squad out after me."

Opara got on the motorcycle and raced off after the nearest of the other two bikers.

"It's just a misunderstanding."

Opara raced up behind the biker, pointed the custom compression gun at the man's brain stem, and pulled the trigger from five feet away.

The gun could have used some fine-tuning on its sight because the pellet went high and to the left. Opara compensated and fired three more times with pellets tearing through the rider's spine and brainstem.

Opara turned and raced towards the remaining member of his hit squad before the man who was missing the back of his head crashed.

The impact didn't go unnoticed by the remaining union hitter who turned his bike and raced toward Opara. The distance between them rapidly closed and it soon became apparent that it had become a game of chicken.

Ajani Opara held onto the handlebars and kept the gun hidden as well as he could manage under the circumstances. The union man didn't even know Opara had it until they were just twelve feet apart. Instead of pulling his weapon and shooting, the union hitter veered left. Opara fired five times, hitting him in the arm, neck, and head as he finally reached for his gun.

The soldier had no idea if the man was dead but his bike had crashed and the man hit the pavement hard. Opara was confident the man wouldn't be getting up to chase after him anytime soon.

Opara rode slowly as he decided on his next step, then saw flames and smoke lighting up the night near the power plant.

Sergeant Ajani Opara rode towards the orange glow.

25

Emissary Thompson quickly realized that the power to her suite had been cut off. She decided it was time to use her wrist communicator to notify the *Behemoth*.

"Sit tight, Emissary. Will send a team in to get you out," Captain Shana Morales said.

"I appreciate that captain. I'll do what I can to try and meet them halfway."

Captain Morales frowned. "Ma'am, I realize you're not in my chain of command, but I strongly recommend you stay where you are."

"Where I am is right smack in the middle of a three-way rebellion. The only use any of these people are going to have for me is as a hostage or to send a message with my corpse. While one is a far better state to be in than the other, I have no desire to be either."

Emissary Sarah Tungsten reached under her robes and pulled out a pair of collapsible shock rods, snapped them to their full length, and held them up for the holo camera in her visor.

"Please correct me if I'm mistaken, but aren't emissaries supposed to go unarmed at all times?"

"A common misconception, Captain. If one reads the fine print in the rules of diplomacy as outlined by the Sway, an emissary cannot carry any weapons of *war*. To my knowledge, shock rods are not used by the military and the constabulary uses shock sticks, a larger version of this self–defense device. Oddly enough, the rods fire off a much larger shock to the system and can shoot shock darts as well."

"The reason the constabulary don't use shock rods is because, on their higher settings, the rods can be lethal and have been known to leave people in a comatose state," Captain Morales said.

"Considering that the governor's forces are armed with

traditional firearms, I cannot see an ethical conflict with using the shock rods."

"Would you be able to use the power from the rods to open the doors?"

"I have the technical knowledge, but I prefer not to waste my power supply. I'll just have them open the doors for me. Please ignore my upcoming emergency signal. Emissary Tungsten out."

The only reason the governor felt comfortable isolating the Emissary in her suite is that he assumed that the communication jammers in effect in the governor's mansion would block any signals she might send out. The man was a fool to not realize that the Sway would have ways around their own technology. Her wrist console emergency rescue beacon broadcasted a carrier wave that went through the signal jammers as if they were nothing but a veil of mist.

Emissary Tungsten sent the rescue message without the cloaking and encryption that her previous communications had used. The governor's people would have to be deaf, blind, and asleep to not notice it.

They were none of these things and several moments later a security team of three men and one woman use a portable jumper pack to open her door.

"Emissary, you're going to need to shut off your beacon immediately," said the woman, a police captain judging by her insignia.

"Why? Has my ride arrived?"

"I'm afraid your ride has left orbit and if you don't shut it down, I'm going to rip it off your wrist."

"An Emissary's band is fused on and cannot just be taken off. It is a delicate surgery."

"I'm not a surgeon or delicate, so unless you want the entire hand cut off, shut it down."

The emissary's legs buckled but she caught herself. "My blood sugar is low. You lot have been starving me."

"Shut it off and we'll bring you some food," the captain said.

"Okay." The Emissary straightened and reached across like

she was going to touch her band screen but instead slid the shock rod out of her sleeve and into the captain's throat. The surge of electricity rendered her unconscious but before she could drop, Tungsten spun and sparks flew as another officer was struck in the face. With the grace of a ballerina who'd taken up fencing, Tungsten dropped to one knee, both arms reeling to the sides to strike the two remaining officers in the legs with the shock rods. The power arced through their uniforms and both men fell to the thick carpet.

Emissary Tungsten paused over the fallen planetary police, staring at their guns.

With a deep breath, she stuck to her metaphorical guns and left the weapons of war in their holsters. Tungsten used the jumper pack to lock the governor's people in her suite. Removing the jumper, she headed toward the next closed door.

26

ergeant Ajani Opara rode into utter chaos. As any soldier can tell you, being in a firefight is hell but the battle zone outside the power plant was a circle of hell he'd never bore witness to before.

It wasn't that three sides were fighting each other. He'd seen that before. It was that the people doing the fighting didn't have any idea what they were doing. There didn't seem to be any real battle plans–other than get inside the perimeter of the power plant and kill anyone else who tried.

The killing part was working but probably not in the numbers any side hoped for.

The governor's police forces had some advantages in terms of training and traditional weapons, but their weapons were designed for peacekeepers. The leaders of the Sway, in their justifiable paranoia, didn't want any weapons available that could match the military because they might fall into the wrong hands, as they had with the Sangre. The congregants may not have had the training but they had the edge on fanaticism over the governor's police who were there for the paycheck.

The real wildcard in the mix was the Granja. While not as fanatical as the blood cultists in their minds they were fighting for themselves and their families which made them more motivated than the governor's police force.

They were also far more creative. Since they didn't have traditional weapons they had designed and built their own, like pneumatic-powered guns and powerful tanks that fired rivets that tore through flesh and metal with equal abandon.

The Grange may have lost their mechs, but what they had was far more destructive. They were cutting through the people with brush hogs and trenchers, basically farm equipment that cleared away brush with spinning blades and a machine with a cab and a giant chainsaw in front of it. They had taken out a couple of mechs with an excavator and a crane with a wrecking ball, then cut off escape using graders to dig trenches in the roads and lawns in a circle around the power plant. The design left only one entry point which the Granja, for the moment at least, controlled.

A tanker with a rigged flame thrower being fed by the tanker-sized pesticide tank had been spitting flames at houses, going down a block slowly to get each one crispy before moving to the next. An entire neighborhood was being devoured by hungry flames.

Opara knew he wasn't going to change the tide of the battle with a single pneumatic pistol and a motorcycle, but he did see a house that was being engulfed by fire. Two children were hanging out of a second-story window. There was a set of parents below trying to figure out how to get them down safely.

Here was something he could help with but first he had to make sure the pesticide tanker wasn't going to turn around to try and finish the job.

Plucking some blankets hanging on a clothesline, Opara folded them over the motorcycle. Next, he raced towards the pesticide tanker rigged to be a flame thrower, firing his pistol at the driver. The cab had metal around it, with only a small slit for the driver to see out of. He climbed off the motorcycle and onto the tanker hood, firing into the slot. He didn't stop pulling the trigger until the man fell over in the cab. He forced the door open, turned off the engine, and closed off the tanker feeder. The flames at the end of the metal pipe went out.

Still, anyone could climb into the cab and start the drivable flame thrower back up.

Among the gear Benedict had outfitted him with was the rest of the detonator shoe. Its sole, like its heel, was made of Z-5. Removing the shoelace triggered a timer and he placed it beneath the tank, then rode away as fast as he could. Ten seconds later, the shoe exploded, turning the tanker into a fireball. The shockwave hit Opara in the back but he kept control of the bike. A glance back told him it destroyed the entire tanker, engine and all.

The soldier rode up to the side of the burning house with the two children in the window. Opara handed the biggest blanket to the parents. "Hold onto the corners."

"They're too scared to jump," the father said. "Even though I told them I'd catch them."

"The blankets will make that easier and safer. I can climb up to the window and toss them down to you."

Every soldier in the Host had to go through basic training which included mastering obstacle courses that seemed archaic for training men and women who would go out on starships. It turned out the training was practical.

It took some doing, but using a lower windowsill and pulling out a few tiles, Opara was able to climb up and get one arm over the sill. The air coming out of the window felt hotter than a furnace.

"Mommy and Daddy have a nice soft blanket below to jump into. Who wants to go first?"

The younger of the pair was a boy who was hugging himself and trembling. He might've been about four Earth years old. His older sister looked about six. While she wasn't trembling, she was holding onto a doll as it for dear life.

"I'm too scared. If we jump we'll get hurt," she said.

Opara hesitated to point out that if she stayed the fire would cook her.

"It'll be fine. Why don't we let your doll go first to prove it." Opara reached in and pulled the doll out of the girl's hands before she could react and tossed it onto the blanket. Below, the mother picked it up and wiggled it in the air to show it was okay.

"Your doll is going to be lonely and scared without you down there so you better be next," Opara said.

The girl nodded and he helped her climb onto the windowsill and get both feet outside. He scooped her up in his free arm and dropped her. She bounced once in the blanket and was quickly enveloped in a hug by both parents. She scooped up her doll from the ground where her mother had dropped it.

The little boy was still frozen in place.

"Your turn."

The little boy took a step back as Opara reached to grab him. All the time he'd been dangling from the windowsill, flames were crawling along the walls of the room and he judged they had less than a minute before was too late to escape the fire.

Swinging his leg over the sill, Opara rolled in, grabbed the boy with both arms, and tossed him out to the window, before climbing back out and dangling from the sill.

The boy was caught and unharmed. Opara hadn't fallen with him because he didn't think the two parents would be strong enough to break his fall.

A blast of heat and fire shot out the window, scorching his fingers and causing him to drop down.

It turns out Opara had been wrong. The parents managed to get the blanket up and catch him. Even though he still hit the ground, the impact was minor. He was bruised but otherwise fine.

"Thank you," the mother said. "Is the rest of the 142nd Starborne coming to stop this?"

"They'll be here as soon as they can but in the meantime, we need to get you and your family as far away from the fighting as possible. Take this motorcycle and go," Opara said.

"What about you?" the mother said.

"I'll be fine."

"How are we all going to fit?" the father said.

"It's all I have, so you're going to make it work."

Opara had the father sit in front with the mother behind him and tucked the four-year-old boy between them. He then lifted up the girl and put her in front of the father so she was facing him. The father took her doll and tucked it inside his shirt.

"You all hold on tight to your dad," Opara said.

With a look of gratitude, the father nodded to Opara. He nodded back.

"I came down North Road and it was empty. If you see any combatants, go off the road and go through the backyards. Don't stop until you are out of the city."

The trencher had turned and was coming across the lawn at them.

"Go!" Opara ran to the side, reached his gun hand in front of the sighting slot, and kept firing until the driver slumped over.

Now it was time to see what he remembered from his time at the Host Academy on guerrilla warfare.

27

"You seem awfully proud of yourself," Private Ricco Jonas said, staring at the short blonde who had been among his three holiday brides, trying to ignore that he was still locked up without a lick of clothing.

"I helped expose a fraud," she said.

"But you didn't. Rutter is still in charge."

"Moron, you're the fraud."

"But I'm not." Jonas realized he was lacking some basic information about the woman who had been left to guard him in the old–fashioned stone cell with the iron bars. "What's your name?"

The woman smirked.

"It's Myna. You didn't seem all too concerned with who I was when you accepted me as a bride."

Jonas nodded. "You're right. It was wrong and that's on me but what you're doing is against Vlad's will."

Mina exhaled and rolled her eyes. "You don't give up."

It was time to lie through his teeth. "Giving up is not the way of blood and I exist only to serve our Dark Lord."

"Rutter told us the truth, that you're no renfield," Myna said.

"You mean Donavan Rutter, the enemy of Vlad that I was sent here to dispose of? Of course, he's going to tell you lies about me. You saw for yourself when the blood font showed who I was."

"Rutter told us how the 142nd hacked into the font to falsely declare you were of the blood of Renfields."

"The blood font comes from Transylvania, built from plundered Martian tech. If it was hacked into, it wouldn't work," Jonas said.

"Then you hacked into the altar lighting system, bypassing the font," Myna said.

"But I didn't. And I can prove it. Put me in cuffs and take me to the altar and watch me put my blood into the font."

"You must think I'm an idiot. You're not getting out of that cell."

Ricco Jonas shrugged, got down, and reclined on the floor. The stone was cold on his bare bottom. "No blood out of my veins. The Dark Lord will free me when he gets here."

Myna laughed. "You think your Major Benedict is Dracula? I guess I was wrong about you. You're not an imposter, you're insane."

"I wouldn't be the first renfield who could claim that but no, I'm not. Benedict isn't the Dark Lord, but he does serve him."

Despite herself, Myna stood up straighter with a mix of disbelief and hope. "Are you saying that Vlad is on board the *Behemoth*?"

Ricco Jonas smiled. She was on the hook and now he had to reel her in without her swimming off into the waters of common sense and logic. "You're no fool and a true believer. Even if he was, I would be forbidden to confirm or deny."

"But Van Helsing and the Sway are said to have killed King Vlad, decapitated him, incinerated him, then scattered the ashes to the four corners of the Earth."

"What else were they going to say? That despite their best efforts, Dracula got away? The Sway had taken over the Earth. How would that have looked? The Dark Lord has been reported to have been killed many times before, yet it never took. We true believers know it wouldn't have taken then either."

"Then how would Vlad have gotten off of Earth during the conflagration?"

"You're assuming he hadn't left his home world. He had Martian ships from way back in 1938 when he led the group that took the fight to Mars and annihilated the invaders of Earth. And who's to say he wasn't the cause of the conflagration, finally wreaking vengeance upon the Sway?" Jonas realized he was laying it on rather thick but judging by the widening of her pupils and the nervous energy she was barely keeping contained, Myna was buying was he was saying. Despite its outrageousness and the fact that he was making it all up as he went along. After all, wasn't the point of all religions to have the faith to believe unbelievable things? He couldn't say whether all religious stories were made up by someone trying to escape death and torture, but he hoped his new interpretation of the Gospel of Blood would be believed long enough for him to escape.

"Why do you think *Behemoth* didn't return to Earth with all the other Colossus class and other battleships? There were enough of us on board who were loyal to our Dark Lord that we took command of the ship and let Vlad's plans come to fruition by not interfering."

"Then why would he come here to Cameroon out of every other colony world in the galaxy?"

"Simple. Transylvania had first became a world power by taking Martian tech as their own. King Vlad knows that in order to rule, one must have superior weaponry."

Jonas let the thought dangle and Myna was kind enough to pluck it out of the air and finish it for him.

"Dracula needs the mechs and the drones!" she whispered.

Jonas nodded and touched his index finger to his nose. "I knew you were the smart one. Rutter was contacted by one of Dracula's servants and the Count Bishop ignored the message, not wanting to give up his tiny bit of power to King Vlad as he swore to do in his vows. The Dark Lord will reveal that he lives on his schedule, but he sent me to test the faithful. Believe me, after this, he will not be pleased with the results."

"Can you prove you're telling the truth?" Myna asked.

"In your heart, you know what I'm telling you is the truth."

"That's great but you could be just feeding me a line of bull. Look at me." Myna moved her hand over her generous curves and exquisite features. "I've looked like this since I turned fourteen. I've had guys telling me stories and lies my entire life so they could get with me. You can understand why I'm a bit hesitant to believe *anything* a guy tells me."

Myna certainly believed the nonsense Rutter had been feeding her about the religion, but Jonas wisely realized it would be counterproductive to point that out.

"You can prove it by putting my blood in the font." Myna started to speak but Jonas held up his hand. "I understand you not wanting to let me out, so allow me to suggest an alternative. Take a sample of my blood with you and put it in the font. The font itself will display who the blood is from so even if the church display was hacked, the Transylvanian-built font would still show the truth."

"And if it says that you do not have a renfield bloodline?" Myna said.

"Then you'll know that Rutter was telling the truth. But if it shows that I'm telling the truth then, you'll know the Rutter is lying to you like every other guy trying to take advantage of you. And worse, that he's betrayed his vows to Dracula."

"You mean like you took advantage of me and your other two 'brides'?"

"I didn't tell you a lie to make that happen. It was the three of you who took advantage of me. I was quite honest with my desire to celebrate the holiday with the three of you and not wanting to take advantage of any of you. How could any human man have said no when the three of you kept pressing me?"

"Fair enough. I'll be back. Do anything to try to escape and I will make sure you regret it."

Myna left and came back a bit later with a traditional hypodermic needle. "Stick your arm out." Jonas got up and did as she requested. Myna stuck the needle in his arm and had to repeat the process several times until she found a vein. Jonas did his best not to flinch or grimace as he was poked and jabbed.

Myna pulled out the plunger and sucked a small amount of blood into the tube.

"Wait here," she said.

"Happy to."

It seemed an eternity until she returned, but he spent the time trying to figure out a way to escape. Naked and unarmed, he couldn't figure out another way other than the plan he was in the middle of or waiting for the extraction team, but they might hurt Myna. Or worse. And he found himself not wanting that.

Myna walked up and placed a hand on the bars and looked

up into Jonas's eyes. Her other hand held his uniform and boots. "You were telling the truth."

"I know," Ricco Jonas replied.

"If I let you out of the cell, what are you planning to do?"

"Stop Rutter and the rest of them from destroying the power plant."

"How exactly are you going to do that?" Myna said.

"Honestly, the plan is a work in progress and I'll probably be making up most of it as I go along," Jonas said.

Myna used an old–fashioned key to unlock the door of iron bars. "What do you need me to do?"

Jonas had been planning to knock her out so she couldn't alert her fellow congregants, but her sincerity made him alter that plan.

"Do you have any fighting training?"

The blonde woman shook her head. "I don't."

"It's will be too dangerous for you out there then. Look, it's possible that we'll lose this battle and Rutter gets back here before I do. I don't want him to punish you for helping me. Let me lock you in the cell. If Rutter finds you here, you can say I overpowered you and escaped. But I will let the Dark Lord know that you are one of the true faithful so that when he chooses to reveal himself, you will be among those rewarded rather than those punished."

"But I'm willing to fight alongside you. To battle for King Vlad."

"And I truly appreciate that but is it not written in the Books of Blood that it profits no one to sacrifice a life that still has value? I want you to stay safe." Ricco Jonas realized that, for at least that last part, he wasn't lying.

Myna stood on her toes and kissed Jonas on the lips. "Thank you. I am honored to have been your bride and apologize for lying to you the way others have lied to me."

Jonas nodded. Myna looked down and smiled. He blushed.

Myna stepped inside the cell and he shut the door with a soft clang. He got dressed before making his way out of the temple just in time to run into his rescue party.

28

The Granja had an advantage and disadvantage all in one. The governor's police force wore uniforms. The congregants of the Sangre were mostly clothed in red and wore necklaces that consisted of a concave arc with an inverted triangle on either side, symbolizing fangs. Each was easy to pick out in a firefight. The disadvantage was anyone not wearing a uniform or the mouth of Dracula was considered an enemy to the other two sides.

The problem–which worked to the Granja's advantage–was that there were a hell of a lot of civilians only trying to flee who'd been shot at simply because they didn't match up with those two sides. It meant that their enemies were wasting time and ammo shooting at decoys instead of actual Granja fighters.

A few dozen people had taken refuge in an in-ground pool trying to stay low enough so they weren't shot but high enough so they didn't drown. It seemed safer than risking the flames of the burning houses all around them. It turned out to be a pretty good hiding spot. At least until spotters from the governor's police and the congregants noticed them.

One would think that someone on either side would have seen the children with their heads being held above water by the adults and realized that these weren't combatants. An all too common mix of fear and adrenaline meant that many of the fighters had given up their normal thought process in favor of adopting a mob mentality. That meant that no one was second-guessing the first person who shouted that Granja were hiding in the pool. The fact that a couple of demolished pieces of equipment lay a stone's throw away only served as unspoken confirmation.

The congregants of the Sangre and the police officers closed in, firing toward the pool. Everyone who could dropped to the bottom under the water, parents pulling children and grown children pulling elderly parents down with them.

The only reason they weren't all outright slaughtered was because it didn't take long for the two sides to realize that the other was firing as well so they changed targets from the unarmed civilians in the pool to their opposite numbers. Three congregants were taken out as was one planetary police officer, but that wasn't enough to make anyone stop firing.

That reason came from above as a military fighter drone dropped out of the sky and fired warning shots at both sides.

"By order of the 142nd Starborne, put down your weapons and lie face down on the ground, putting your hands on top of your head. Failure to obey will result in you being fired upon," came a voice through the drone's speaker.

"Go screw yourself!" came the reply from the speaker of one of the planetary police force P-1 mechs as it fired on the drone, knocking it from the sky. The right arm of the P-1 aimed at the people in the pool. "If you're not with the governor, then you are the enemy!"

"And you just made the wrong choice," came the voice of Corporal Luiz Cardosa through his speakers. Unable to hear anything over the sound of his engine and speakers, the police mech pilot hadn't noticed the pair of black military mechs that came at him from either side. Cardosa launched a rocket-propelled grenade at the P-1's nearest knee joint, blowing it to smithereens and knocking the blue mech down so that its shots at the pool went high.

Before the police pilot could aim at his new target, the second mech stood over him and used a mechanical leg to stomp out its other knee joint while using its heavy steel fists to pound on the pilot's canopy door.

It took just over three minutes to tear it open. The police pilot threw his sidearm out and raised his hands above his head, surrendering.

Three more drones dropped out of the sky flying in a back-and-forth pattern, their weapons pointed in the direction of the combatants. They repeated the message that the first one had made. This time they all surrendered and placed their weapons on the ground.

The prisoners were ordered to move together so the drones could guard them while the two X-1 mechs stood on opposite sides of the property scanning for combatants amid the streets and burning homes.

"Harpy Alpha Nine, you're cleared for a battlefield landing," Corporal Luiz Cardosa said into the con system. The dropship landed, crushing somebody's garden beneath it.

The ramp dropped. Inside there was already a good size group of people including a family of four that stood next to a motorcycle and a woman with a metal visor and black robes.

A dozen armed soldiers marched out, ten reinforcing the perimeter the gaps in the perimeter the mechs had made. The other two went to the edge of the pool.

"Hi folks, I'm Sergeant Lucille Durango, but you can call me Lucy. I need all of you to get out of the pool and head into the dropship as quickly as possible. I ask that those of you who can help those who might need a little more assistance."

"Sergeant Durango, we have hostiles approaching in construction equipment," one of the soldiers on foot said.

"Roger that, Private Phuong. Corporal Cardosa, do you think you and your X-1 could run some interference for us?"

"It will be my pleasure," Cardosa replied from inside his black mech as he marched towards the approaching members of the Granja.

"Folks, this is going to become unpleasant very shortly so I need you to double time into the dropship," Sergeant Durango said.

She and Private Phuong bent down to help pull people from the water, who when on dry ground turned to help pull others. Sergeant Durango went out of her way to smile at anyone who looked scared, which was pretty much everyone.

As they approached the ramp, the woman in a black hood and robes stood at the top and smiled as she greeted the rescuees. "Welcome everyone to Harpy Alpha Nine. I am Emissary Tungsten and I'm here to assure you that despite the violence and chaos ensuing outside, the soldiers of the 142nd Starborne have everything well in hand. You will all be taken outside the city where we have set up a refugee center where you'll find food and shelter. If any of you are aware of any of your fellow citizens who might be hiding somewhere and are also in need of rescue, please let us know immediately. If any of you are armed, you have one moment of amnesty right now to raise your hands above your head and let the soldiers know that you need to be disarmed. If you take advantage of this now, you will not be harmed. If you are found with a weapon after this moment, you will be treated as an enemy combatant. Let me assure you of two things. Anyone on board who has a weapon and is not a member of the 142nd Starborne will not leave the ship alive. And two, everyone on board will be scanned. No weapon will remain hidden for long." The Emissary was using her visor to help the soldiers using a scanner. "Please line up against that wall so you can be scanned before joining the rest of the rescued further back. Thank you."

A man lifted his dripping arms and held his hands above his head as he turned towards a soldier. That soldier and two others approached him and removed a pneumatic gun from the small of his back. He was led to a different section of the ship where guards were watching over a few other people.

Sergeant Lucille Durango and the other eleven soldiers who exited the dropship with her stayed on site while another dozen soldiers moved into position at the door as the ramp raced up into the closed position.

Soldiers on the ground ran out of the way as the harpy lifted off to reach the next group of people who needed to be taken out of the battle zone.

29

Sergeant Cardosa had become comfortable enough with the X-1's controls to be able to get his mech moving at a quick jog. There was always a risk in doing that with a machine with legs because, despite the strength and durability of any mech, all it took was one small miscalculation for the machine to trip and fall over. While there was an auto-right function, it didn't always work and even when it did, it could take several moments until the mechanical footing was regained. A fallen mech was at its most vulnerable.

Cardosa was fortunate that he kept his footing and even fired a rocket-propelled grenade at a brush hog that was bearing down on a group of armed police combatants. It was driving far faster than the people could run and they were seconds away from dismemberment when the RPG took out the brush hog's blades. The shockwave stalled the farm equipment's engine. Cardosa fired a second grenade RPG at the cab and the driver drove out just in time to survive but just slow enough to lose some hair and skin to the fiery blast.

"Throw down your weapons and surrender," Cardosa ordered through the speaker system to the armed combatants who had stopped running and started firing at him. None of the police force or blood congregants' weapons had the firepower to do more than take a chunk or chip his armor but not every attack was designed to kill the enemy. Sometimes it was just meant to distract.

Corporal Cardosa realized that the instant after the wrecking ball smashed into the back of his mech, crushing the middle and knocking him down the street where the X-1 landed on its side.

The wrecking ball struck the X-1 two more times, each hard enough to embed the mech into the pavement, breaking three of his four limbs and cracking his pilot's canopy.

"I'm down and under attack," Cardosa screamed into his comm, but he became silent as the chainsaw from a trencher pressed against his cracked canopy.

His last working mechanical limb was the machine's left arm. It still had one RPG left, but firing from this distance would catch him in the blast and the canopy wasn't intact enough to protect him from the blast. The armor–piercing rounds were in his useless right mechanical arm.

Cardosa worked his controls so the left mechanical arm reached up and wrapped its three mechanical fingers around the chainsaw and squeezed. The chainsaw kept buzzing so he squeezed and pulled as hard as he could. The chainsaw cut through the bottom finger just as he tore the buzzing engine of destruction partway off the trencher.

However, the damage was done. The protective canopy was gone and he was rushed by a mob of the governor's police officers who fired into the cockpit. Corporal Cardosa wore body armor but he had removed his helmet in order to pilot the mech. That is where the governor's forces aimed.

The soldier's life ended with the contents of his skull splattered all over the cockpit.

The second military mech rushed toward him once she heard his cries for help but was too late. Private Karen Hansen fired high-caliber armor-piercing rounds that tore through the police armor as if they were paper. They paid the price for killing her fellow soldier but their deaths did nothing to calm her anger. She fired a single armor piecing round at the driver of the wrecking ball and it tore through the cab's makeshift armor as if it were silk. Several of the police who has rushed the canopy were fleeing on foot. Hanson used the mech's targeting system to take each of them down with a single shot from her right arm. She raised her left mechanical arm and fired RPGs at every piece of industrial equipment in range, incapacitating them and killing or wounding all of their drivers.

A blue police mech and one of the crimson mechs decided to put aside their differences long enough to attack Hansen in her black X-1.

Private Karen Hansen didn't bother firing a weapon. She knew the difference between their specs and hers. Both were faster but neither matched her armor or offensive capacities.

When the police mech got close enough, Hansen reached out with both mechanical arms to grab hold of the outside of the blue P-1's shoulders and pulled laterally while squeezing through the joints with the blades embedded in her mechanical fingers. After a struggle, both metal arms tore off at the joint. Hansen used both blue metal arms as clubs on the police mech, landing rapid blows worthy of a boxer.

First, she smashed the canopy and then went to work on the legs. The police mech collapsed. Private Karen Hansen lifted her right mechanical hand and brought the torn arm directly down on the shattered canopy, crushing the pilot into lumps of uniformed meat and jelly.

Deacon White, who was piloting the crimson mech, saw the display of skill and brutality and turned his tank with legs around and ran as fast as his mechanical legs could carry him. Hansen activated the hydraulic leap function of her mech. It was limited to three uses but Hansen didn't care. The X-1 soared over the top of White and the crimson mech to land in front of him. The private proceeded to use the two mechanical arms the X-1 was holding to give Smith the same treatment she'd given the planetary police officer. In moments both the deacon and the mech were out of commission permanently.

Hansen turned but the fighting was far from over.

30

"Attention ground troops, this is Captain Patel," the harpy pilot said over the comm system. "You have three groups of incoming hostiles approaching the power plant. I estimate numbers in excess of four thousand."

"Damn, we didn't bring enough ammo," Sergeant Lucy Durango said.

"If we stand and fight, it'll be a massacre. At least at the start," Private Hansen said.

"And then we'll all die when we run out of ammo," Sergeant Durango said.

"We're not going to let any of those things happen," came Captain Shanna Morales's voice over the comm. "Complete the search and rescue of civilians and get back on the dropship."

"Yes ma'am," Sergeant Lucy Durango said.

"You don't mind my asking, ma'am, what are we going to do after that?" Private Karen Hansen said from inside her X-1. "As near as we can tell, all three factions have forces inside the walls of the power plant. The thing's nuclear. If they should damage the core…"

"The fusion core can stand up to a cluster bomb and that place is only putting out helium instead of radioactive waste. As long as the fuel stays in the pod, everything will be fine."

"And if it doesn't?" Private Hansen asked.

"We could be looking at a dirty bomb situation, not a nuclear blast. It's more the converter that I'm worried about. If they destroy that, it could be years until a replacement could be gotten."

Depot was the main site for the manufacturing of mechs and drones. Converters for civilian power plants were built on another world entirely. All colony fusion power pods needed to be hooked to a converter to power a city. The converters had a self–destruct that the Sway could engage should a colony become rebellious without risking an environmental disaster with the fusion pod. When the colony got back in line, they'd be given a new convertor. Ship pods, like the one from the Titan class cruiser, didn't have this feature as it was a bad idea to leave a ship that vulnerable. "As for our next steps, Major Benedict has decided that he's going to go and speak with the approaching combatants about considering alternative courses of action."

"Ma'am, from down here, I have to say these folks don't appear to be in much of a talking mood," Sergeant Durango said.

"Benedict can be very persuasive," Morales replied.

31

"We have the firepower to wipe them all out, Hans," Colonel Zhang said on a private channel.

"I'm well aware, Bai, but we are supposed to be in the business of helping people, not slaughtering them," Benedict said.

"If we were still following Sway policy for the Host, we would be ordered to engage at least a small portion of each section of this revolution with an overwhelming show of force and firepower and let the corpses of their fellows frighten them into submission," Morales said.

"Which is why this never would've happened before the conflagration. We took over command of *Behemoth* with the intention of being better. I don't see how killing all these people aligns with that philosophy," Benedict said.

"A fact for which I remain grateful, Hans, but there are thirty-six thousand people in that city. How can we allow four thousand to put the other thirty-two in danger?" Zhang said.

"We can't."

"We can't put it off any longer. What do we do? Set ourselves up as rulers of the planet? Take it over like we did *Behemoth*?" Morales said.

"We have neither the desire nor the experience to do that," Benedict said.

"So which one of these three factions do we set up to run the government?" Morales said.

"None of them have the citizens' best interests at heart," Benedict said.

"Hans, what government ever has? We need to start looking at which would be the lesser evil," Zhang said.

"No. We have an opportunity here; one I think is unprecedented in human history. We can help guide this world to become the first true democracy."

"Hans, not to contradict you but the Greeks technically were," Zhang said.

"Not a true democracy. Only wealthy men got a vote. Women, servants, and slaves were all left out of the process. We have the technology to give every person a chance to vote."

"History teaches us that in republics where people only had to vote maybe once a year, very few countries achieved even fifty percent participation. If the majority doesn't participate, it rather ruins the point," Zhang said.

"True so we find a way to enforce voting. Double taxes for nonvoters. No access to government services."

"So we'll be forcing them to abide by our decision on what their government should be," Morales said.

"No. Well, yes, but we will be forcing them to make their own decisions and listen to what they decide instead of what we tell them," Benedict said.

"I suppose that is slightly less fascist," Morales said. "But you know as well as I do that people like the Count Bishop and Union President Taft will do their best to influence and force others to vote the way they want."

"So we write safeguards into their Constitution to minimize that," Benedict said.

"Now we're writing their Constitution for them?" Zhang said with an amused lilt in his voice.

"We'll want this ratified quickly so it seems logical to do the heavy lifting for them," Benedict said.

"What if they decide they want to change things?" Zhang said.

"We put the ability for them to amend things right in the document. We get rid of the politician class and instead have administrators whose time on the job is limited. We forbid lobbying and quid pro quo. We provide an open forum where anyone can speak on the planetary network."

"This sounds like a very complex document."

"It will be, especially since it will have to have it in plain language so the average citizen can understand it," Benedict said.

"And just who were you planning on getting to write such a historical document?" Zhang added under his breath, "As if I didn't know."

"Bai, I was hoping you would head up the project, recruiting anybody and everybody on board who you think can help," Benedict said.

"I do so love a challenge. When would you like this completed?" Zhang said.

"Twenty–four earth hours if it's not too much of an imposition."

"From your voice alone, I can't tell if you're being sarcastic or serious," Zhang said.

Benedict chuckled. "Both, although I think we can probably get a bit more time, but it will be best to have something to offer the masses to consider as soon as feasible."

"If not sooner," Zhang said.

"Exactly. Anything else as I'm about to try and head off four thousand armed and angry dissidents," Benedict said.

"Just you in a mech suit?" Zhang said.

"Nah. I'm bringing backup."

"Good. I'd hate to have to pick up your job duties in addition to my own."

Both men chuckled but Morales said, "We all know I'm carrying the lion's share of the day-to-day running of *Behemoth*, so I'll tell you now, I'm not taking on anything else so don't die."

"Yes, Shana," Benedict said.

"There is one other thing. You might be amused to know that Daily has been demanding to speak with you every time he sees a guard. Apparently, he is not pleased with his roommate situation," Zhang said.

"Pity for him because we don't need his code anymore," Benedict said.

"There are however many other bits of intelligence it

would benefit us to know. Would you mind if I negotiated with him for those?"

"Not in the least, Bai. I think it might be best if we worked together to get every last bit of intelligence out of that sanctimonious bastard."

"We'll visit him when this is done. Good luck with not having to slaughter any of the dissidents."

"Thanks. Benedict out."

32

The approaching foot soldiers for the three rebellious factions all seemed to learn about the location of the others at the same time and adjusted their courses accordingly. The Granja fielded the most people, with the governor's forces in second, and the congregants of the Church of Blood coming in third.

What the Sangre were lacking in numbers they made up for in fanaticism. There weren't enough guns for all of the Granja or the Sangre so they had gotten creative using everything from spears, bows and arrows, and modified gardening implements. Each of the governor's police forces had more guns but their ammo was limited which meant in any prolonged battle they were going to have to fall back on chemical sprays and shock sticks and eventually use their batons.

Major Hans Benedict had done his best to figure out where the three forces would encounter each other and was only off by a few hundred feet. As the citizens of Depot prepared to kill their fellows for the benefit of their leaders, Benedict marched his black mech between all three groups.

"If I can have just one moment of your time before you proceed with killing your friends and neighbors," Major Hans Benedict said with his speakers at maximum volume. "I have a solution that could prevent a whole lot of senseless killing and dying, but for this to work I'm going to need to see Governor Cardell, Union President Taft, and Count Bishop Rutter over here for just a moment."

The citizen rebels all stopped and looked awkwardly around as nobody stepped forward.

"I guarantee your safety," Benedict said. "So please just step up, even just to the front of your troops if you're too nervous to come over here."

There was some murmuring among the crowds.

"Are your leaders not here?" Benedict said. Many in the armed crowd shook their heads. "But that doesn't make any sense. Real leaders, at least ones who care about those following them, would be in the heat of the battle alongside their followers. Are you telling me that instead of being here with all of you brave folks, they are cowering somewhere safe? How could they do that while all of you whom they are bossing around are risking your lives? They must be something special for all of you to be willing to die just so they can hide far away from the danger they sent you to face. Me? I'd never follow someone like that," Benedict lied. He'd spent a career having to follow the orders of men like Daily who were happy to send others out to face down the Reaper when the scariest thing they'd have to face that day was their meals getting cold before they ate them. "I mean, I'm the head of the 142nd Starborne but I'm right here."

"Safe inside a mech," shouted one of the Granja troops.

"Excellent point but I'd be far safer on the bridge of the *Behemoth* in orbit, now wouldn't I?" Benedict said.

"Hey, I resemble that remark," teased Captain Shana Morales on their private channel.

Ignoring his second-in-command, Benedict said, "What kind of gutless wonders orders others to slaughter and die in their name and doesn't have the balls or the decency to even show up? I believe the technical term for that is a chicken shit coward."

The crowd murmured, looking at all the others who were there to kill them or be killed by them.

"Your leaders are willing to throw away your lives in a bid for personal power." Benedict turned to the police forces. "If the governor wins, you all get to keep your jobs but that idiot couldn't even pay you. The 142nd Starborne had to step in and do that. In fact, we won't be paying any rebels next week, so if you choose to fight anyway, you'll be killing your friends and neighbors for free. If Cardell wins, and any of you survive, what do you get? Nothing that you don't already have now. I bet you that craven coward didn't even promise you all a raise."

Some of the police nodded.

Benedict turned to the Granja union workers. "You were all promised you'd own the means of production. Really? You all understand basic economics–if you spilt it up evenly, none of you will own much of anything. But Taft gets to decide who gets what. Ask yourselves, is Taft going to put those factories and farms in your names or his name?"

A few muttered, "Taft's."

"Exactly. You'd only be trading the old boss for a new one. And the bastard could have just given you the food he stole, but instead, he *sold* it to you. What kind of union member does that to a fellow member of the Granja? Not someone who deserves to be in the union, let alone president of it. And the union members who survive are going to have to do more work. You know why? You'll have to pick up the slack from the dead Granja members."

More muttering from the crowd. "Taft said we won't have to do work no more!"

"None of you were foolish enough to believe that line of bullshit, were you?" More looks and murmurs. "Where would the replacement workers come from? Even if you put every wealthy person to work, that would equal maybe five of ten percent of your workforce, right? And they wouldn't have the skills to do it right. There would be no crops next year to harvest and everyone on Cameroon who survives this mob-killing Taft, Rutter, and Cardell are ordering you lot to do, will starve. Taft won't want to starve, so if none of you are going to be working, who is going to work his factories and farms? Zombies?"

Some worlds actually embedded mechanical controllers in the brainstems of the walking dead and used them as a labor force. Benedict couldn't imagine anything stupider than allowing carriers of a deadly plague to work among people but the Sway hadn't asked his opinion.

"None of you would allow that, which means after you kill everyone Taft wants dead, you will all go back to work in his farms and factories, but you'll have to do more work. Why? Because a lot of you won't survive tonight, let alone the weeks and months ahead in this mob fighting. You'll have to pick up the slack for your dead friends. So you'll all be murderers and none of you will be promoted to owners of anything except the guilt of having killed your friends and neighbors so Taft could live out his dreams of becoming a rich bastard. Good luck sleeping when the faces of those you kill come back to haunt you in your dreams." Benedict spoke from experience.

The major's X-1 turned towards the congregants of the Sangre Temple. "Count Bishop Rutter has betrayed the principles of the Books of Blood. Dracula was at the front of every battle his country ever fought starting with the Battle of Transylvania in 1918 where he alone defeated the armies of both the Kingdom of Romania and the Austria-Hungry German Empire and made them give him back his country of Transylvania and then some. Dracula would never hide away from this battle like Rutter. He would be here, boots on the ground, alongside all of you. If Rutter had behaved like this as a general in Transylvania, King Vlad would have staked him as a coward and a traitor, yet you follow him in defiance of Dracula's ways? You're not here killing in Dracula's name. You're killing in the name of the spineless weakling Rutter."

Rumblings came from within the crowd of congregants.

"They lied to you. We never left orbit. We found out what happened to the missing ordnance. You've all heard about it?"

There were some scattered nods in the crowds.

"They weren't missing. It turns out your leaders conspired with Jonathan Tark, some local rich guy. Tark bribed the governor to look the other way. Taft took a bribe to get the ordnance out of the factory. Rutter took his bribe to arrange delivery of the mechs to Tark at his country manor. Tark was planning to sell some of the mechs and drones to AWOL soldiers in exchange for the activation code and keep twenty or so for himself to set himself up as the new ruler of Cameroon, all while telling each of your leaders that he supported them. We've got video of Tark and messages from him telling your leaders that we had left orbit and that they should take control of the power plant. Tark wanted all of you to weaken and destroy each other, making it easier for him to step in and take control of the colony with his ordnance."

"You're lying!" yelled a police officer.

"Then how did all of you just happen to get marching orders to attack the power plant in the middle of the night? Wouldn't your leaders normally have planned for something this big? Did any of you know about the attack before you received a call in the last few hours?"

No one spoke up that they had.

"Doesn't this seem suspicious to all of you? It's a lot to take in, but I came here to propose an alternative to death and bloodshed. I propose you form a new government, one without leaders, only administrators who serve for a short time. We can set up technology so that each person on this world gets to vote on laws and rules rather than voting for a person.

"So instead of trying to kill each other to better people who only pretend to care about you, you get to vote to make real changes in the laws and on your colony."

"What if they decide they want to get rid of our religion?" shouted one of the congregants of blood.

"None of you will be able to do that. Your Constitution will grant you certain inalienable human rights which will include freedom of religion but it will have clauses that will prevent you from enforcing your religious beliefs on others. You'll be able to worship how you like unless that worship infringes on the rights of others."

"What about when the rich try to take advantage of the working class!" shouted one of the Granja.

"I'm sure they'll try but there are provisions in the Constitution that will limit what they can do. It includes rules on safe working conditions, reasonable hours, and sensible pay," Benedict said.

"What about if these lots decide they no longer want police protection?" shouted one of the planetary police force.

"Police protection will be guaranteed in the Constitution but there will also be penalties for the abuse of that power. Toward that end, it will include mandated body cameras but that is to protect the police from false claims of brutality as much as it is to protect the public from abuse of power."

"It sounds like you've addressed everything we're fighting for," shouted a Granja worker.

"We tried. And if we missed anything there are provisions in the constitution where a two-thirds majority of the citizens can change certain things. Basic human rights however are unamendable."

"What if we decide we don't want you imposing this on us and we all take you out?" one of the congregants of blood asked.

"I've given you all the opportunity to live through the night without either dying or becoming killers. If you all decide you'd rather be murderers and slaughter each other, that is your decision. However, be aware that the 142nd Starborne stands to protect the citizens of Depot caught in your crossfire. That means the lot of you can go out of the city limits into a field and kill each other to your heart's content but I will not allow any of you to endanger innocents who are not involved in your fight," Benedict said.

"You think you can stop all of us with one mech?" one of the planetary police said, a threat dripping from each syllable.

"Yeah. We built those suits," one of the Granja said. "We know their weaknesses."

Benedict let the bluff go. There were no magic buttons to press to stop the mechs.

"There are thousands of us and only one of you," one of the congregants of blood shouted.

"I assume you were paying attention earlier when I said that I as a leader was at the forefront of this battle. You must not have understood that means I'm not alone, only in front of my people." Benedict lifted the arms of his X-1 and motioned dramatically to his sides. "142nd Starborne, move into position."

At Benedict's words, dozens of newly activated black military mechs stepped out from the houses they were hiding behind. The air above the rebels filled with drones. And in the skies above the drones hovered twenty Harpy dropships.

The rebels began to panic as they looked at the massive display of firepower that surrounded them on all sides. Laser sights in the arms of each X-1 and a few X-3s wove and danced among the crowds, more for dramatic effect than targeting, but it was effective.

"If any of you move against my people or the citizens of Depot, we will open fire and mow you down. We will not allow your groups to further destroy people's homes-"

Dropships and X-1s were trying to contain the blaze to the neighborhoods around the power plant.

"-or to murder innocent people. We stand between you and your future war crimes. Each of you has a decision to make. Choice number one will be to lay down your weapons on the ground, turn around and return to your homes in preparation for your chance to become part of a new government where you will all have an equal voice. Choice number two is to decide that you think it would be best to try and kill each other outside of the city. Choice three will be to ignore your good sense and survival instincts and try to make war in this city for which, I guarantee, you'll die in the process. If you choose choice two, we will follow you out to make sure you are only harming each other. Anyone who puts all their weapons down will be under our protection, the same as the other uninvolved citizens. Anyone who still has a weapon will be escorted to that field. I recommend choice number one. Do that right now and we will let this matter drop."

"What about our leaders?" shouted one of the Granja. "Do they get off scot-free?"

"Not at all. I have something special in mind for them that will settle this whole conflict once and for all."

Benedict told the rebels his plan. Murmurs of approval rumbled through the crowds.

"You guarantee that will happen?" one of the planetary police said.

"As long as none of them are dumb enough to commit suicide, you have my word that is the plan," Benedict said.

The planetary officer nodded and placed his gun and

weapons on the ground and turned to leave. The rest of the planetary police officers followed suit, some with more reluctance than others, perhaps worried that their opponents would not do the same. Next, the Granja put down their weapons, stepped out of their equipment, turned, and left.

Last, the congregants of blood lay down their weapons and left.

Major Hans Benedict clicked off his speakers and let out a huge sigh of relief.

33

Pandemonium would have been an improvement compared to the situation inside the Depot power plant. At the door to the central plant which housed the fusion pod, the three rebel forces were doing their best to kill anyone who wasn't on their side.

A congregant of the Church of Blood was at the power chamber entrance and picking off anyone who approached. A member of the Granja crept up behind another of the Sangre who wasn't watching his six and put a pneumatically launched pellet in the back of his head and into the wall. She then removed the dead man's red shirt, the color of which camouflaged the former owner's blood quite nicely. Next, the Granja member removed the corpse's mouth of Dracula necklace and put it on, then sprinted down the corridor. She hoped that the congregant wouldn't notice she had stolen her too-large red outfit until it was too late. When the Granja member got close enough, she put a pellet between his eyes then was shot in the back with a pellet from a fellow Granja member who was also fooled by her outfit. Unsure of his skill and aim, he had fired ten pellets. Number six had hit his fellow union member but the third, fourth, and fifth tore through the waste tube from the reactor which collected valuable helium released by the fusion reaction which was then used in the factories for welding and in the compression tanks among other things. The helium byproduct from the fusion pod was released into the air.

Once her corpse hit the floor, no one was left guarding the door. The entrance was rushed by members of all three sides firing wildly at each other. There were some hits but none of them fatal so three police officers, four Granja, and two congregants made it through the door.

All nine quickly realized that except for the reactor pod, there was nothing in the power room to take shelter behind. The fighters each tried to group up with other members from their side while wildly moving their weapons back and forth in a mixture of fear and attempted intimidation.

"Put your weapons down. You are all under arrest," shouted one of the planetary police force, but instead of the booming voice of authority he had planned, his voice was high-pitched.

"I don't think so, squeaky," said one of the Granja, whose voice came out just as high-pitched. "You can't arrest us anymore! It sounds like you haven't even hit puberty yet."

"The helium lines must have been breached," squeaked one of the congregants.

"We're just lucky it wasn't the fusion generator," squealed another member of the Granja.

"They say that the generator pod is designed to withstand high caliber weapons and small explosions," another of the planetary police officers said.

"But was it made on a Monday morning or Friday afternoon? If it was, the quality might be off or the workers could have missed something," squeaked another member of the Granja. "With all of us this close, I really don't want to test its armor out."

"Tritium has a short half-life," countered the squeaking planetary police officer.

"A dozen years isn't that short and we're all standing right here. Would exposure kill us with cancer or radiation sickness?"

None of them were scientists but they all knew the horror stories of the nuclear disasters in the days before the Sway controlled the Earth. It was enough to make all of them hold their fire.

"So what do we do?" squeaked one of the Granja. "Stand here and give each other dirty looks?"

"We have the rightful authority and we outnumber you." The planetary police officer reached to the canister on his belt as did the other three. "And we have weapons that won't risk damaging the generator pod."

The two men and one woman in the police uniforms sprayed the faces of the six opponents and followed that up by using their shock sticks to knock them out, then passed out themselves as the helium they were inhaling stopped their bodies from being able to absorb oxygen.

A police mech smashed through the wall next to the door.

"We control the power plant!" came a voice from the P-1's speakers.

It was hit from behind by a crimson mech, knocking its metal belly first onto the floor. The Sangre pilot opened fire with its arm on the unconscious police officers and Granja members.

The crimson P-1 positioned itself in front of the generator pod as the police mech initiated the auto–upright feature and pushed itself into standing. The police pilot swung his metal arms at his crimson counterpart. The Sangre pilot spun around in time to get her P-1's arms up to block the police attack. The walking tanks grappled, evenly matched since, with the exception of an extra coat of paint, they had identical specs. They might have stayed locked in that position wrestling if the armored mule vehicle hadn't rammed into the police P-1 from behind, knocking both mechs over and onto the converter interface, crushing it into hundreds of pieces.

34

"Hans, the power just went out in the entire city of Depot and the majority of the outlying homes and farms," Captain Shanna Morales said over their private comm.

"Dammit. Just when I thought we had a chance of pulling this thing off without any more hitches," Benedict replied. "We need to take control of that power plant and see if we have any shot at getting it back online."

"From our intelligence on the ground, it seems a blue and red P-1 tore through the building itself without regard for structural integrity in hopes of being the first ones to the generator pod," Morales said.

"Idiots. It's not a child's game where the first one to touch the pod gets to keep it. Now that we are at full strength and then some with ordnance, I don't want any soldiers on foot entering the grounds."

"Understood," Captain Morales said.

"Send in drones to map the place out then send in X-1s."

"Same engagement protocol?"

"Yes. Minimal. Avoid killing locals if possible but not at the cost of the safety of even one of our soldiers or civilians. How's the other prong of our attack shaping up??" Benedict said.

"All three extraction teams are in position to begin at the same time so that none of the targets get any advance warning by hearing about what happened to their opposite number," Captain Morales said.

"With the sudden power outage, they may be on guard, thinking we had something to do with it," Morales said.

"Maybe but I don't think so. This is due to the bumbling of one or possibly all three of the rebel forces and we can assume that are getting reports," Benedict said.

"They are and we've been monitoring all messages. Lieutenant Yun used each faction's communications to triangulate their leader's whereabouts. We can jam their communications at any time."

"Hold off on that, especially if it's helping us,"

"Nice job talking down all three groups of infantry by the way."

"Thanks. Time will tell if it just bought us time or if it worked. Let me know when the extractions are complete."

"Don't you mean if?"

"I'm choosing to be optimistic here."

"I noticed. It's a tad out of character, but I like it. We'll do our best to not let you down. Morales out."

35

The strike team for the governor got the go order and rushed through doors that had been unlocked for them by Emissary Tungsten.

The governor's security forces pushed him to the back of the room, opened an escape door that looked like a regular wall panel, and pushed him and one of his security detail through it. The pair made their way through the dark escape tunnel which let them out in an unused apartment in the building next door. As they stepped into the apartment through another disguised wall panel, the guard preceded the governor. The armed man was greeted with a shock dart to the neck and crumpled twitching to the floor.

Before the governor could flee back into the tunnel a shock rod was placed against his throat.

"Unless you want to join your security man on the floor there, I suggest you don't move," Tungsten said.

"Emissary, it's most unseemly of you to threaten me with weapons," Cardell said. "I am the Sway governor after all."

"It was far more unseemly for you to take me hostage. By the way, you're no longer governor. By the power vested in me by the High Council of the Sway, I hereby remove you from office."

"You have neither the right nor the authority to–"

"The authority was granted to me by the same people who made you governor. If my power is no longer valid then neither is yours. Either way, civilian, you have a fun day ahead of you."

One of the half-dozen soldiers holding rifles waiting alongside the Emissary took the ex-governor's wrists and bound them behind his back.

Cardell's foul-mouthed response was very much beneath the dignity of his former office.

36

The union safe house turned out to be badly misnamed. Using heat sensors that gave a picture of everyone in the building, the extraction team cut a hole through the roof, dropped onto the floor of the second story, and sliced another hole in that. A soldier in full body armor repelled down to grab Union President Taft around the elbows and chest. In the dropship hovering above the holes the end of the soldier's safety line quickly retracted bringing the soldier holding Taft up into the bay of the dropship, with the rest of the extraction time being reeled in right behind them. The harpy was in flight before any union members could even react.

Count Bishop Rutter had been coordinating his forces from the relative safety of a congregant's basement, far away from the power plant and the fighting. They had electric lanterns with them and were keeping track of the congregants in the field using radios and a map they had carved into a wooden table.

The church members would have all confessed that the teargas had taken them by surprise but that the fired beanbags that knocked them to the ground truly shocked them. Beanbags even took out the electric lanterns.

Soldiers of the 142nd Starborne equipped with gas masks and night goggles using use both infrared and sonar walked through the smoke-filled darkness to pluck Rutter up off the floor and drag him out to the waiting harpy .

38

The three faction leaders were tossed unceremoniously into the center of a circular fence made from livestock wire attached to posts that rose over three meters in the air.

"What's going on?" Union President Taft demanded. "Are we being imprisoned? If so, I will file a grievance!"

"This is a violation of my religious freedoms. I demand to be released immediately!" Rutter shouted.

"It is unconscionable that you should do this to a duly appointed representative of the Sway," former governor Cardell bellowed.

"Sorry, Cardell, but you know as well as I do that Emissary Tungsten removed you from office for unfitness and dereliction of the duties of your office. As for you, Rutter, religious freedom doesn't excuse you from following the rules of society. And Taft, feel free to file a grievance if it will make you feel better," Benedict said. "You'll have to file it with me by the way."

"This prison will never hold me," Rutter said.

"This isn't a prison," Benedict said.

"Then what is it?" the former governor demanded.

"An arena."

"Why would we be in an arena?" Taft said.

"Three of you decided to fight a war and endanger not only the people fighting for you but innocents who wanted no part of your shameful grabs for power. We have hundreds dead and thousands homeless because of you three. That is unconscionable," Benedict said.

"That's a bit of a hypocritical position for a soldier to take," Rutter said.

"I disagree. No one understands the stupidity of war like a soldier who has been in one. I've always felt it was wrong that the rich and the powerful force the poor and young to fight their battles for them. Thanks to the idiocy of you three, I've been given the opportunity to do something about that. Instead of your followers and troops doing the fighting, it's going to be the three of you battling it out. Last one standing will be crowned the winner."

"You're being hypocritical yet again, Benedict. You lead a side in this conflict yet you're out there," Rutter said.

"I hate to admit it but the bloodsucking preacher has a point. What gives you the right to stand out there?" Taft demanded.

"The fact that I won, but I'll make you three a deal. I'll be happy to step in and take on the winner if it will make the three of you happier."

The three men looked first at Benedict then at each other. The major was in his forties with a bit of gray around his temples but was lean and well-muscled. The three men's assessment of themselves was that they were overweight and out of shape. None of them was likely to beat Benedict in a fight, fair or otherwise.

Before they could express their feelings on the matter, Benedict continued. "Consider it done. In the meantime, do whatever you need to win."

"There is a huge flaw to your plan, Benedict. We could all simply choose to not play your game or fight each other," former governor Cardell said.

Benedict nodded. "Of course, but that shows your followers the type of men you really are."

The three leaders looked around and saw nobody but armed and ready soldiers of the 142nd Starborne.

"What followers?" Taft said.

Benedict pointed to cameras placed at various points around the inside of the wire arena. "Jonathan Tark played you all for fools so he could take over the colony. Following his machinations, the three of you bumbling at playing war and have destroyed the power plant's convertor and plunged this world into darkness.

"However, the colony's satellites are still working and most people have self-powered tablets which will work until those charges run down. We've preempted all three entertainment channels and the learning library so that all anybody can watch right now are the three moronic cowards who have thrown Cameroon back to the dark ages. They know you all demanded your followers fight, kill, and die for you. And now you show them that this was because you were all too weak and pathetic to do your own fighting. The only difference between today and yesterday is now everyone on the planet knows what kind of men you are."

"I'm no coward!" Taft said, slamming his fist into his chest. The other two men dropped back into a defensive stance as they all sized each other up.

Rutter was the first to make a move, charging at the former governor with his hands held up like they were claws and his mouth opened, showing his dentist-designed fangs.

Cardell got his forearm up so Rutter bit down on his sleeve. Cartel responded by bringing his knee up into the preacher's groin. Rutter bent over with the pain but focused through it and tried to scratch the ex–governor's eyes out.

Taft had grown up doing hard manual labor. He was a decade-plus removed from doing any kind of physical work but was still bigger than the other two. Taft came up behind Rutter and kicked his foot into the preacher's knee. The pain made the Count Bishop let go of Cardell in an effort not to buckle.

One didn't rise through the Granja ranks to be elected president without having a sense of showmanship. Taft grabbed hold of Count Bishop Rutter by his collar and his belt then lifted him up, intending to bring him over his head, but only had the muscle power to make it as far as his shoulders.

Bringing one of his knees up, he slammed the religious leader's spine down onto his leg. Rutter's back cracked and the preacher started screaming. Taft tried to throw the preacher's body but it ended up being more of a drop.

The former governor charged before the bigger union man could turn to attack him. Since it had worked on Rutter, he tried the same method of attack on Taft bringing his foot up into the union president's groin from behind. The big man doubled over in pain and Cardell smashed him in the cheek with a fist. It would have been more effective if the former politician had learned how to throw a punch. The blow hadn't done much more than stun the union man, but it managed to get him to focus through his pain. Spinning around and reaching up, he grabbed hold of Cardell's lapels and pulled him down so the former governor was pinned under the bigger man's body weight and proceeded with pounding his face with his fists.

Taft knew how to throw a punch and pummeled the smaller man despite Cardell's attempts to bring his arms up to ward off the blows. A dozen punches later, Taft was winded and Cardell's face was battered and bloodied as unconsciousness claimed him.

Taft rose to his feet extending his hands over his head in triumph. "I win. I am the new leader of Cameroon!"

The makeshift wire gate creaked open and Benedict stepped inside the makeshift cage. "No, you're not. Cameroon is going to be the first true democracy in human history."

"Then what was all that for?" Taft motioned with his arms to the unconscious Cardell and the moaning Rutter who was unable to move his legs.

"I told you. This fight was to end this nonsense between the three of you and save your followers from having to kill and die to feed your egos and hunger for power. And to show the people of this world who you three are. Now as you requested, you get to fight me."

Full of adrenaline and drunk on his victories, Taft charged Benedict.

The sapper stepped to the side and stuck a leg out, tripping the bigger man.

"That was sad. Is that the best you've got?" Benedict said.

"I'll show you what I've got." Taft sprang to his feet and came at Benedict swinging. The major was already moving backward and slid to the side of the first punch, then a second. The third punch that came was much slower. Benedict grabbed hold of the big man's pinky and bent it back along with his wrist, breaking the finger and flipping the man onto his back. Benedict kicked the union president beneath his jaw, knocking him unconscious.

Benedict turned towards the nearest camera. "Now you all know what kind of losers were trying to carve this world up as their personal kingdoms. Cameroon is better than them. In two days, we should have everything set up for all of you to vote using your retinal scans-" All in the Sway database. "-through any electronic device on the planet. All three channels and the library will be displaying the Cameroon Constitution, giving all of you a chance to read it over and then vote on whether to rule yourselves or let more morons like these three try. I know each of you knows in your heart that any of you could've done a better job than any of these three. So look over everything and ask questions. Be informed. Members of the 142nd Starborne will be available to answer your questions both in person at key locations and via the communication system. As I mentioned, these three with the help of Jonathan Tark destroyed your power converter and your batteries will run out of power soon. The 142nd Starborne will try to find a replacement. In the meantime, we have recently come across another fusion generator pod from a starship that does not require the converter interface. Our engineers will be working through the night to attach it and restore power to the colony. This generator is not a gift but a loan. In exchange, the 142nd Starborne is asking for some things to be manufactured for us, as well as a regular supply of fresh fruit, vegetables, meat, and spices. You will be able to vote on whether or not our asking price is acceptable. I am letting you know upfront if it isn't we will be taking the power pod with us. Either way, we will be working towards getting you a replacement converter so you will no longer be dependent on us but we hope to lay the groundwork for a barter system between us going forward. I envy you this chance to be the first colony to rule themselves."

39

"They ratified it with almost 72% to become a democracy," Captain Shayna Morales said.

"I'm more impressed that they had over 94% participation," Colonel Bai Zhang said

"Did anyone try to game the system?" Major Hans Benedict said.

Zhang nodded. "More than a few, but all of them unsuccessful. Now we have a crucial decision to make. We left a back door in the system just in case there were issues. If we leave it in place, we will be able to change any voting in the future that might be against our interests," Zhang said.

"It could come in handy," Shayna Morales said.

"And also undercuts everything we're trying to accomplish. If we can just swoop in and change the will of the majority of people on Cameroon, does that make us any better than the Sway High Council?" Benedict said.

"We're alive, so that makes us better right off the bat," Morales said with a grin.

"Regardless of that, we would not be doing it for personal gain, so we would be better in that respect as well, but using the High Council as an example is hardly setting a moral high bar. Ethically, we would be wrong. Plus, if we leave a backdoor, it makes the system vulnerable. Once we seal the door, there will be no way for anyone to alter it without everyone on the planet knowing. With the back door intact, eventually a hacker will figure out a way to game the system," Zhang said.

"Then the three of us are in agreement. We slam the voting system back door and fuse it shut," Benedict said. Morales and Zhang both nodded. "You'll take care of it, Bai?"

"I already did," Zhang said.

Morales smiled. "What if we had decided otherwise?"

Zhang chuckled. "Captain, please. There is no way this vote

could have gone otherwise."

"Also on the win side, Cameroon voted to ratify the contract with us for the loan of the titan generator pod. Not nearly as high as the ratification overall, but those in the city of Depot voted to accept it by over ninety–five percent. I guess they didn't like being in the dark. The constitution also mandates how food distribution is to be handled in times of crisis so we won't have people rebelling just to feed their families in the future."

"Excellent, so we will be able to supplement our meals with fresh food as the meat Rushmore gifted us after we prevented the globs from destroying their herds has finally run out. And we've also managed to farm out some larger repairs?" Benedict said.

"Mostly components for harpies and some other areas of the ship, but yes," Morales said.

"Considering the intrinsic value of the titan pod, I recommend we leave behind a platoon, a half–dozen drones, and four X-1s to provide security. Plus, a couple of engineers to keep it up and running," Zhang said.

"Before this, I never could've imagined leaving behind that many mechs. Then again, our full contingent would've been twenty before. Not counting Private Hugh, we lost eight mechs to the globs. Now we have an embarrassment of riches. Speaking of which, we now also have an Atlas class freighter. I suggest we go into the transport business. The colonies need something reliable to transport their imports and exports and not gouge them in the process," Benedict said.

"One freighter won't fix everything but if we have a squad of furies go as escort, it will reduce the risk of pirates. And we can focus on food, medicines, and other crucial supplies," Morales said.

"We can't spare a squad. Maybe one. A pity we don't have more," Zhang said.

"What's the status of our rebellion leaders?" Benedict said.

"Count Bishop Rutter died of his injuries. Cardell was beaten to a pulp but should eventually recover much of his function. Taft has a broken finger and jaw, but should be healed in six to eight weeks," Captain Morales said.

"I guess you went a little too easy on him," Zhang said with a smirk.

"I got my point across."

"We took custody of Cardell, Taft, and Stark before the new democracy existed so we don't have to worry about extradition. We certainly don't want any of them imprisoned on the same world where they have so much influence. We don't want to be called back here in a year or two because they managed to talk their way out of prison and started another rebellion against this infant democracy."

"The union will be holding a vote to elect a new president. There will be no new governor but the staff will be retrained to work for the democracy. The police force will be gone through with as many of them being kept as feasible, but the ones who can be proven to have committed war crimes, along with members of the Granja and the Sangre, will be tried by the new democracy. That of course leaves us with who is going to take over the Sangre Temple."

"Private Jonas had a solution for that which I approved," Major Benedict said.

40

"What our church is going through right now is difficult, having been led so far astray by the heretic Rutter," Jonas said. "As per the rules laid out in the Books of Blood, as the highest ranking member present here, it is up to me to appoint the next Count Bishop." Ricco Jonas had been sorely tempted to claim the top spot for himself but decided power would corrupt, although he would sorely miss celebrating the festival of the brides. Maybe he could arrange leave for the holiday.

In fact, most members of the congregation assumed he would appoint himself the new Count Bishop. From what he heard, the congregants were split down the middle as to whether or not they thought that would be a good thing.

"After much deliberation, I decided that I will pass on claiming the spot for myself and continue our Dark Lord's mission by serving aboard *Behemoth* with the 142nd Starborne."

Holding his hand over the font, Jonas pricked his finger, allowing a few drops of blood to fall. The font again identified him as a renfield.

"By the power vested in my bloodline through Vlad, King of Transylvania, and lord of blood, I hereby appoint Myna Walers as the next Count Bishop. She has shown courage in serving the Dark Lord and is the most worthy of this position. Serve her as you would serve one who serves Lord Dracula."

Myna rose from the congregation and walked up to the altar as two male deacons brought the tailored crimson robes of office and put them on her. She wasn't the first female Count Bishop in the church's history but it was still far from common. There would be challenges ahead.

After the service, there were greetings and congratulations from the members of the congregation. After that, Myna and Jonas retired to the sacristy.

"I'm still in shock over you naming me Count Bishop," she said.

"I told you that you would be rewarded for your loyalty."

"Why hasn't Lord Dracula revealed himself? Why would he allow this colony to become a democracy instead of bowing down and serving him?"

Jonas had embraced the deception and made Major Benedict aware of it. They both figured it was better for the colony and for the 142nd Starborne to have the head of the Sangre Temple on Cameroon feel friendly towards them than otherwise.

"His mind is not mine to know. All I've been told is he is not ready yet to reveal himself and he feels a democracy will allow people to rule over themselves instead of being ruled over by someone who is not him. To be truthful, I don't know if he will choose to reveal himself in our lifetime. I also don't know that he won't. All I know is that I will continue to serve him like my great grandfather before me."

"And I'm still not to share this news?"

"Such is the will of Vlad."

"I am certainly going to do my best to make things a lot better around here. And I think at least for the festival, I'm going to insist that men be allowed to become 'brides' as well as women."

Jonas laughed. "I don't blame you one bit."

"When do you have to return to *Behemoth*?" Myna said.

"I have some flexibility. We won't be shipping out for at least a few weeks. We are helping rebuild the neighborhoods destroyed by the fires. Why?"

"I was hoping you might consider staying with us until it's time to leave."

"As long as it's not back in that cell."

They both laughed.

"I was thinking more along the lines of staying in the Count Bishop's chambers," Myna said reaching up and wrapping her arms around Jonas's neck.

He wrapped his arms around her waist. "That sounds like a fantastic idea."

41

Daily was laying on the bottom bunk of the three. He had started out on the top but Robiten and Holland had forced him onto the bottom.

Robiten and Holland were sitting in chairs and using a third chair as a table to play cards on. It had been Daily's seat but the other two men had taken it away and pushed him off onto the floor or worse every time he tried to sit there.

The former general eventually had given up and either sat on his bunk or in the corner of the room.

Daily had been wrong. His life had gotten worse. The toilet was in the cell and even that was a nightmare. He had to beg the other two for a scrap of toilet paper since the bidet was broken. He suspected Benedict had arranged that on purpose.

The other two men forced him to act as their servant— making their bunks, serving them their meals, and scrubbing the sink and the toilet with his toothbrush.

He had tried appealing to their honor as soldiers but as far as he could tell, the men no longer had any. He accepted that there might be some resentment over their fates; he had served for decades with soldiers resenting him, but he never had seen anything like this.

He realized that without the chain of command, he was too old and weak to make someone obey him. He contemplated ending it all, but he wasn't about to give that bastard Benedict the satisfaction.

It hurt to admit it, even to himself, but Benedict had broken him.

When he returned, he would tell him the activation code. Not right off the bat of course. He'd negotiate, get better, solo accommodations. Some punishment for Robiten and Holland went without saying. Better food. A real mattress.

"Gentlemen, it's exercise time," said one of their guards. The hour they got each day to exercise for their only time out of the cell. His only time to avoid his two former subordinates who had made his daily existence a living Hell.

Robiten and Holland were fitted with shock and knock collars in case they tried to escape. The collars injected a knockout drug and gave an electric shock. They were taken out to the exercise room. For some reason, they hadn't put his collar on.

A moment later, Daily realized why when Benedict stepped into view, with Zhang following behind him.

"Hello, Daily."

"Benedict. Zhang. Come to see our little bit of paradise," Daily said.

"Your definition of paradise must be quite different than mine," Benedict said.

"We've seen the cell surveillance feed," Zhang said.

"How's life on the bottom bunk?" Benedict said.

Benedict and Zhang then let the silence between them grow. It was an old trick. Be quiet and let the person you were facing speak to fill the silence. Three could play at that.

Benedict and Zhang weren't playing. They turned to go.

"Wait."

Benedict turned. "Yes?"

"I'll tell you."

"Tell us what?" Benedict said.

"What you wanted to know last time we spoke."

"Nah," Benedict said.

Zhang shrugged. "We're not interested anymore."

"Nonsense. You're not the type of men who give up. I'm willing to trade. To start will, I get my cell back to myself. Then I want…"

"Nope. You waited too long. Your information no longer has any value," Zhang said.

"We all know for what you lot are doing with the 142nd having X-1s, X-3s, and fighter drones will make your command much easier," Daily said.

"They have."

"What do you mean they have?"

Benedict gave a fake smile.

"You are full of shit. The Inspector General was on Earth as was anyone else who knew. Without me, that ordnance will stand and rust."

Benedict shrugged. Zhang smiled.

"Look, Benedict, you always keep your word. You said if I told you if you'd give me back my cell to myself. The activation code is 9 1 Alpha Zulu Echo 7…"

"4 Bravo 8 Whiskey Foxtrot…" Benedict said.

"Quebec Tango 4 Uniform 7…" Zhang added.

Daily's pupils grew four sizes. "You know it!"

"Yep. And here you are neither dancing or naked, although I'll concede your current situation may be Hell for you."

"How?"

"Sorry. Classified," Benedict said and held up his shock collar. "I'll extend your exercise period by the length of this conversation."

"No. Wait. I know other things."

Zhang shrugged. "Nothing that means anything to us."

"I know the override to the Host discretional fund."

"The mark isn't worth what it used to be," Zhang said.

"I know more activation codes!"

"To what?" Benedict said.

"Harpies! Furies! At some point you will need more ships," Daily said.

Benedict and Zhang exchanged a look. Benedict leaned in and whispered into Zhang's ear, then the colonel returned the favor.

"We could use those," Benedict said.

"And you will get rid of Robiten and Holland?"

"From your cell," Zhang said.

"And I want a proper bed," Daily said,

The pair exchanged a look and then nods.

"Fine in exchange for all three codes, you get a bed and your own cell for three months," Benedict said.

"Wait? What do you mean three months? I'm giving you tritium here. I deserve my own cell. I'm a five-star general, damn it!"

"You were. Then you were willing to kill your entire crew and a hundred thousand colonists because the people who killed billions on Earth snapped their fingers and told you to come running," Benedict said. "And the original deal was for permanent solo accommodations but you turned that down. We needed the ordnance activation code. We don't need those other codes, just want them," Benedict said.

"The way I figure it, each month you will need to offer us something of value to keep living alone," Zhang said.

"That's inhumane," Daily said.

"No. Putting people in situations that are not good for them is sadly all too human," Benedict said.

"So do we have a deal?" Zhang said.

"I don't think so," Daily said.

"Sergeant Lank, how long until Daily's roommates come back?" Benedict asked a guard.

Lank looked at a clock on the wall. "Forty-three minutes, sir."

"Enjoy your forty-three minutes to yourself," Benedict said.

"Forty-two now, sir," Lank said, trying not to smile.

"Thank you, sergeant."

Daily's throat let out a low growl. "Six months."

The major and the colonel exchanged another look and nod.

"Four months," Benedict said.

"Five."

"Seventeen weeks and one day per month of non-vat meals," Benedict said.

"Deal," Daily said through gritted teeth.

Daily gave them the three codes.

"It goes without saying that if these turn out to be phony, there will be consequences," Benedict said.

"It does."

"We'll clear their belongings out of the cell while you get your hour of exercise," Benedict said as Zhang put Daily's shock and knock collar on him. The guards took him to the exercise room.

"That went well," Benedict said.

"It did. Although the meals were a generous touch, do you think he'll realize that in ship's time, four months is 17.2 weeks and that he accepted 33.6 hours less time than your previous offer?" Zhang said.

"I do," Benedict said. "And it's going to tear him up inside."

There has long been a debate among certain obscure and drunken literary scholars about whether **PATRICK THOMAS** was raised by Cthulhu, a leprechaun in a Manhattan bar, or two human parents. What there is no arguing about is that Patrick is the award-winning author of 40 books including the beloved fantasy humor *Murphy's Lore series* (9 books from *Tales from Bulfinche's Pub* to *The Mug Life*), as well as 2 books in the future space adventures in the *Startenders* series.

The Murphy's Lore After Hours spin-offs star the half pixie/ogre Terrorbelle (*Fairy With A Gun, Fairy Rides The Lightning,* and *Terrorbelle The Unconquered*); the former demon-possessed serial killer Agent Karver of the Department of Mystic Affairs (*Dead To Rites, Rites of Passage*); the cursed magí Hex (*By Darkness Cursed* and *By Invocation Only*); Vince Argus, the Soul For Hire (*Greatest Hits*); and Negral, a forgotten Sumerian god who works as Hell's Detective (*Lore & Dysorder, Bullets & Brimstone,* and the graphic novel *The Moon Maniac* with Blair Webb).

His *Mystic Investigators* paranormal mystery series includes *Shadows & Brimstone* (omnibus of *Bullets & Brimstone* and *From The Shadows* with John L. French), *Once Upon In Crime* (omnibus of *Once More Upon A Time* and *Partners In Crime* with Diane Raetz) *Mystic Investigators,* and *Mean Streets. Assassins' Ball* is his first traditional mystery, co-written with John L. French. He co-edited *Camelot 13, New Blood, Hear Them Roar* and was an editor for the magazines *Fantastic Stories of the Imagination* and *Pirate Writings.*

His other works include the steampunk *As The Gears Turn.* the space epic *Exile & Entrance,* and the *Bikini Jones* series. Patrick's darkly humorous advice column *Dear Cthulhu* has been running since 2005 and has 6 collections including *Cthulhu Knows Best* and *What Would Cthulhu Do?* The Dear Cthulhu advice empire has expanded from magazines and books to radio as Dear Cthulhu now broadcasts monthly on the show Destinies: The Voice of Science Fiction which is hosted by Dr. Howard Margolin.

Over 100 of his stories have been published in magazines and anthologies. His noir novella appears in *Murder in Montague Falls.* A number of his books were part of the props department of the *CSI* television show and *Nightcaps* was even thrown at a suspect's head. His urban fantasy *Fairy With A Gun* had been optioned for film and TV by Laurence Fishburne's Cinema Gypsy Productions. Top Men Productions has turned his *Soul For Hire* Story, *Act of Contrition,* into a short film.

He also writes books for kids as PATRICK T. FIBBS including the YA *Emotional Support Nifghtmare,* the midde readers *Undead Kid Diaries: Over My Dead Body, the Babe B. Bear Mysteries: Bad Hair Day, Joy Reaper Checks Out,* the picture book *Fushcia The Mermaid Who Loved Pink,* and *the Ughabooz* picture books *5 Silly Monsters Jumping On The Zed* and *On Top Of A Yeti,* and the early reader *Soggy Goes to the Beach.*

Please drop by www.patthomas.net or follow him at I_PatrickThomas at Twitter or www.facebook.com/PatrickThomasAuthor to learn more.

The Past, Present, and Future of the Abyss!

The Inspirations for the
Rising Storm: The Starborne card game

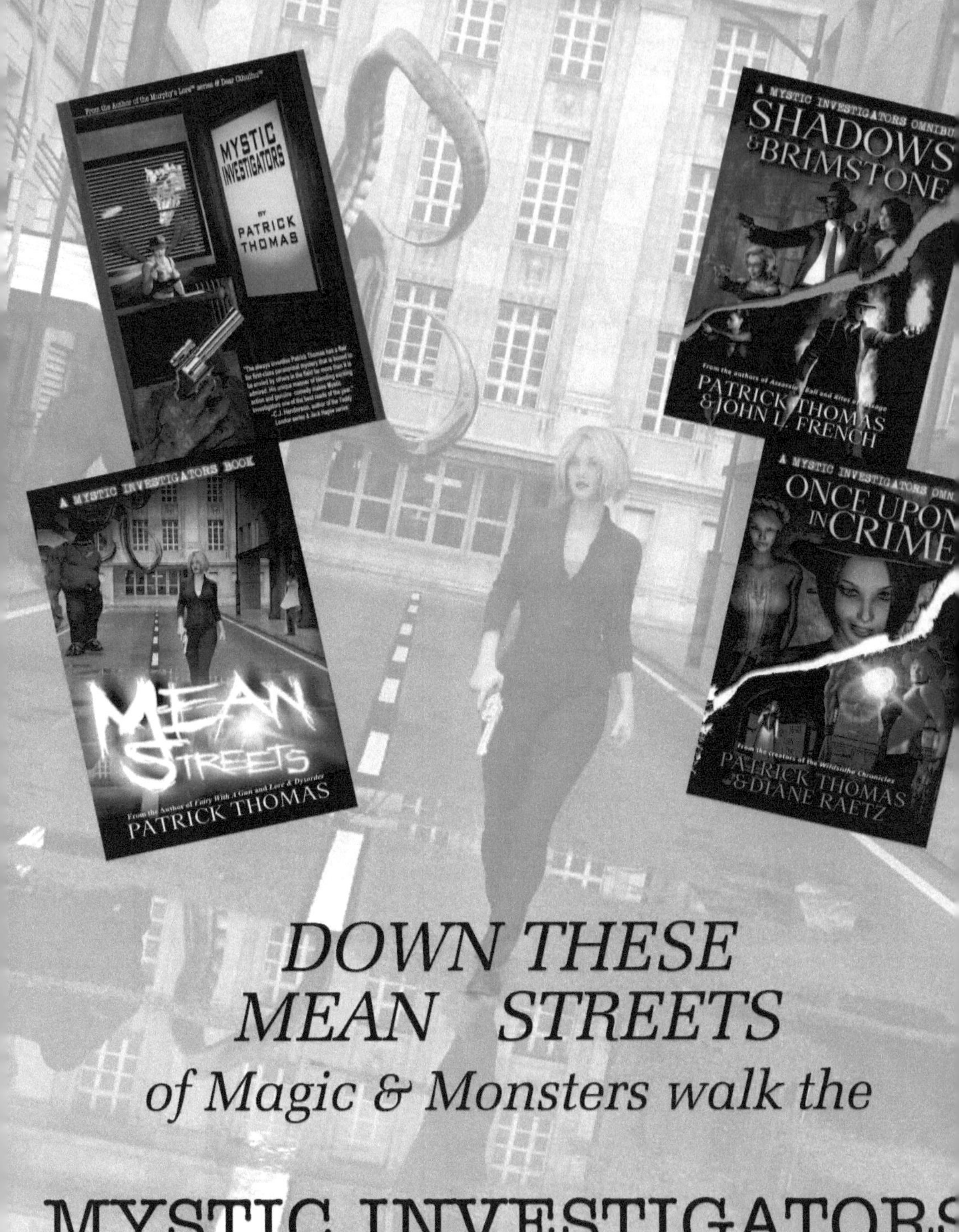

DOWN THESE
MEAN   STREETS
of Magic & Monsters walk the

MYSTIC INVESTIGATORS

**Being *CURSED* to wear a bikini
Won't stop this Hero
From *SAVING* the world**

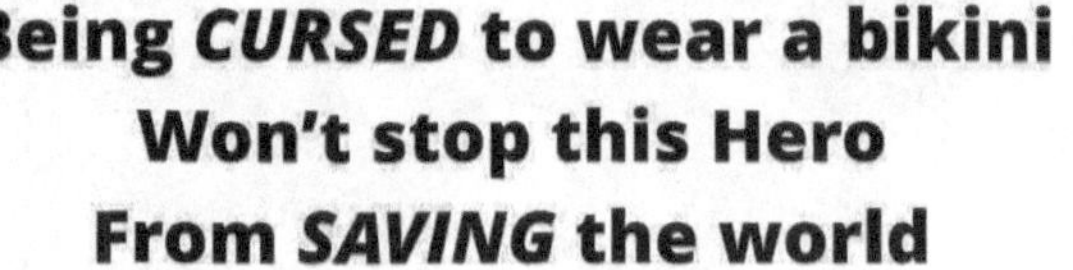

**THE ADVICE
COLUMN TO
END ALL
ADVICE COLUMNS**

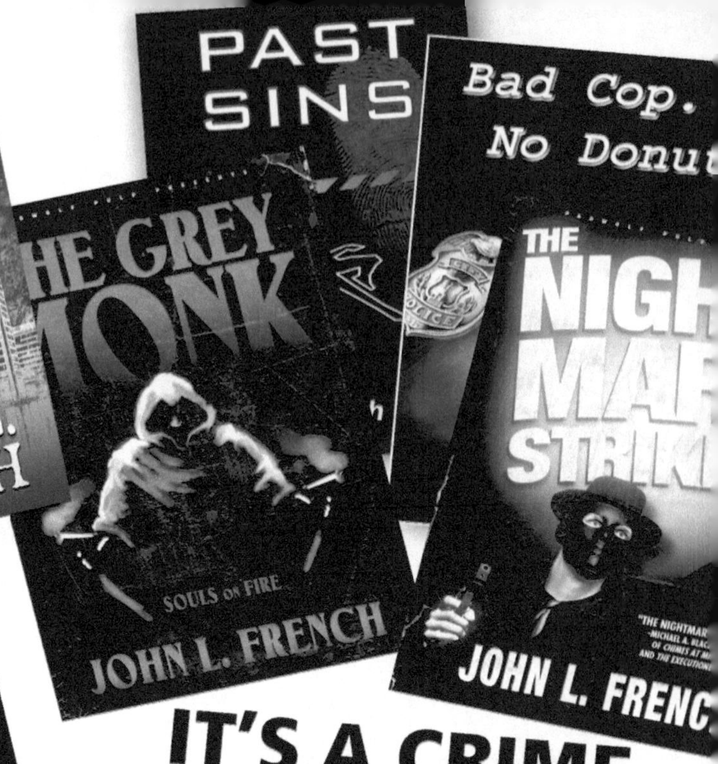

Welcome to the Freakshow!
Monsters Among Us
a Bianca Jones collection
PAST SINS
Bad Cop. No Donut
Welcome to Baltimore!
Here There Be MONSTERS
a Bianca Jones collection
THE GREY MONK
SOULS ON FIRE
JOHN L. FRENCH
THE NIGHTMARE STRIKES
JOHN L. FRENCH
JOHN L. FRENCH
JOHN L. FRENCH
IT'S A CRIME TO MISS THESE GREAT STORIES!
from author
John L. French
WWW.PADWOLF.COM
You can't get better than 13!
APOCALYPSE 13
DEFCON 1
TALES FROM THE MERMAID
Camelot 13
Edited by John L. French and Patrick Thomas
LUCKY 13
Edited by Edward J. McFadden

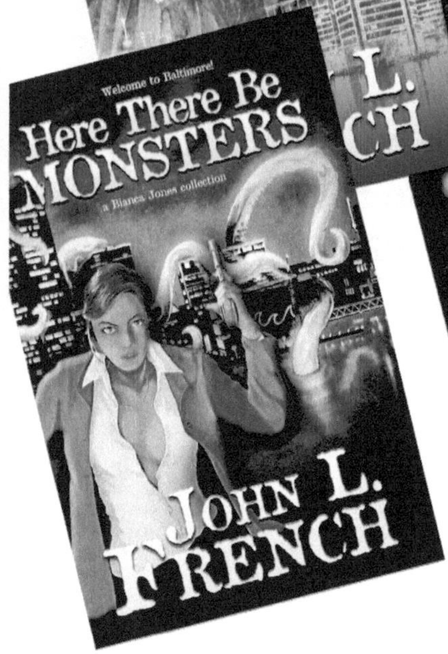

More GREAT Science Fiction!

THE STARSCAPE PROJECT

As his quest begins, an artificial intelligence life form enters the galaxy and launches a series of covert attacks against the Empire. The Teconeans assume that the Federation is responsible, and galactic peace is about to unravel. As Stryker chases his nemesis into Teconean space, he finds himself thrown into the middle of the battle. Knowing that Earth will be the aliens' next target, Stryker must decide whether to let them destroy the Empire, or to join forces with his Teconean enemies against the invaders. The key to the mysterious aliens lies buried on the moon of Kennedy Prime, and it's up to Stryker to solve the puzzle before war begins. The fate of the galaxy is at stake.

ZONE OF THE TENTH DGREE

In 1912, an alien ship crash lands in the Atlantic ocean, setting up a secret colony that remains undetected for centuries, allowing them to manipulate some of the most important events in human history -- from the sinking of the Titanic to the Bermuda triangle to global warming. Now, the technology of the 26th century has discovered the aliens' distress beacon, and it's a race against time as the Navy tries to stop a terrorist armed with a nuclear weapon from destroying the colony and triggering an all-out war as the mother-ship approaches

Now available from

Shape up...
You only get
ONE Warning

Hell's Detective

No One Is Above The Lo
Even In

Help is only a Rainbow Away…

"Mix Gaiman's American Gods and Robinson's Callahan's Crosstime Saloon on Prachett's Discworld and you get an idea of Thomas' Murphy's Lore." -David Sherman, author of STARFIST and Demontech

"ENTERTAINING, INVENTIVE AND DELIGHTFULLY CREEPY." -JONATHAN MABERRY, New York Times and Bram Stoker Award Winning Author

"SLICK… ENTERTAINING." - Paul Di Filippo, ASIMOV'S

"HUMOR, OUTRAGEOUS ADVENTURES, & SOME CLEVER PLOT TWISTS." -Don D'Ammassa, SCIENCE FICTION CHRONICLE

PATRICK THOMAS

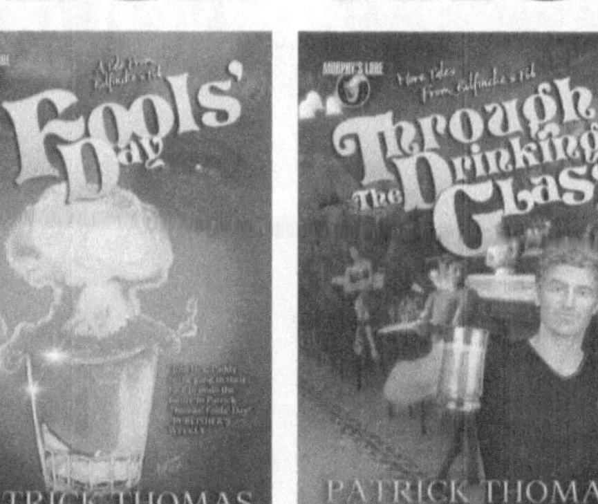

Features all
6 books in the series in
one deluxe volume!

NO TEACHERS.
NO PARENTS
SCHOOL IS OUT....
OF THIS WORLD

www.talehaven.com

EVEN THE TEENAGE
QUEEN OF DARKNESS
NEEDS A FRIEND

EMOTIONAL
SUPPORT
NIGHTMARE

PATRICK T. FIBBS

One Last Chance to Save Happily Ever After

an a group of heroes including Goldenhair, ed Riding Hood and Rapunzel help General now White and her dwarven resistance ghters defeat the tyrannical Queen Cinderella? nd will they succeed before a war with /onderland destroys everything?

heir only hope to stop Cinderella's quest or power lies with a young girl named atience Muffet who carries the fabled hards of Cinderella's glass slippers.

oy Mauritsen's fantasy adventure iry tale epic begins with *Shards f The Glass Slipper: Queen Cinder.*

"Fantastic...
A Magnificent Epic!"
-*Sarah Beth Durst* author of
Into The Wild & Drink, Slay, Love

"The Brothers Grimm
meets
Lord Of The Rings!"
-*Patrick Thomas,* author
of the Murphy's Lore series

"Shards is a dark, lush,
full-throttle fantasy
epic that presents
a bold re-imagining
of classic characters."
-David Wade, creator of
319 Dark Street

"Roy Mauritsen's
enchanting epic
comes at a time
when fairy tales
are back in the
forefront of
our collective
imagination."
-Darin Kennedy,
short fiction author

In paperback & e-book
Find out more at:
shardsoftheglassslipper.com
padwolf.com